MW01644811

Of Onyx and Light

D.L. Spitznogle

Of Onyx and Light

D.L. Spitznogle

ISBN-10: 1536918989
ISBN-13: 9781536918984

The amazing cover art for this book was created by:
Daniela @ SelfPubBookCovers.com/Daniela

Author's Note

The wonderful little town of Kathrine, Iowa is a fictional town. However, it is based on a real town, Grandview, Iowa, that sits not far from the location of Kathrine. Kathrine exists between the real towns of Muscatine and Wilton, and I'm sure the wonderful men and woman farming that land won't mind if I borrow some of it to bring you this story. Gale is another fictional town that also requires me to borrow a bit of farmland for its existence.

In short: I've taken the liberty of altering the world to suit my needs.

I would like to dedicate this to my wife, Kortnie. Your constant support of my writing is amazing. I couldn't have made it this far without you.

To my children, for keeping me strong and focused.

To Jessie, because of your hard work, people believe I can actually write.

Prologue

It was just past midday, and the desert sun beat down from its perch high overhead. The scorching sand blew harshly against the small house. Walls made of mud and straw protected the inhabitants from the sandstorm that could strip flesh from muscle and muscle from bone. The home was settled in the desert far to the west of Nazareth with the Sea of Tiberias a half day's walk further to the east. Despite the unusual dryness, heat, and unrelenting sandstorms, the man they sent for made the journey in three days. His knocking could barely be heard over the wind.

The man waiting outside was wrapped in a dusty gray linen robe. It was worn thin in spots and beginning to fray. His sandaled feet were submerged in the sand as he stood in front of the door. Protecting his face from the harsh sands was a swatch of linen wrapped around his head and neck. His companion, dressed in black linen robes, walked their camels to a small barn several yards from the house where he led them inside for their own safety. He was glad to see that there was at least a little water at the bottom of a trough and even more glad that he talked his companion into riding the camels instead of the donkeys they were accustomed to.

Sticks and split logs held together by fiber from palm fronds made up the door, and it quietly squealed an exhausted sigh as it opened. A short woman stood in the entrance; her eyes were red from crying. Her black hair hung in a way that matched the sadness she wore in her expression, but she smiled wide and cried with joy as she saw the man standing outside her humble home. She had never seen him, yet she heard many tales of his greatness. "Praise God, you have come."

She urged the two men inside, closing the door behind them. With the harsh elements locked outside the men lowered their hoods. The man in front was in his mid-twenties. He had long dark-brown hair and a short beard. His brown eyes were filled with kindness and patience, and his smile seemed to light up the room. With him was a man with black hair that was slightly lightened by the sand stuck in it. He appeared to be tired and slightly impatient as if he were being inconvenienced.

"I am Jesus of Nazareth. This is my good friend and companion, Judas Iscariot," Jesus spoke. His gentle voice was confident and commanding "We have heard of a sick child. She is sick beyond help?"

"My name is Karam. Please, come this way. My home is your home." The woman led the two men through a small family area that consisted of a wooden table, several chairs, and a fireplace.

Judas, feeling famished after the long journey, grabbed a handful of dried dates as he walked past the table, an expression of delight marked his face as he bit into the sweet chewy fruit.

"It's my daughter, Adina. She has slept most of the day. That is until right before the storm hit. She moaned and sung a wretched song, stopping moments before you arrived. She has been this way for days. My husband has taken our son with him to Capernaum to sell our pottery. I have asked him to take his time in hopes of you curing Adina before their return."

"We will see her immediately then," Jesus said. Not only did she notice the kindness in his words, but she admired his confidence.

The temperature dropped significantly as he walked through the hanging linen curtain that separated the girl's room from the family area. The light mist of their breath hung in the air for a moment as if it were a ghost making its presence known. Judas pulled his linen hood back up over his shoulders as the chill crept through him. He sensed something else in the chill other than the cold, and he could smell salt with a hint of mildew. He examined the window: it had been shuttered with wood and palm leaves, and he turned his attention to the candles. Their flame's provocative dance felt unnatural to him. Swaying seductively, trying to invoke lust, but he would not succumb to this demon's trickery.

On a small straw bed in the corner of the room rested the young girl. She was seven years old. Too young to go through this torture, Jesus felt, but then again, no one should have to face this evil. Her small body lay straight under the wool blanket. Her face was an image of perfect calm. Her eyes were shut. Long brown hair swept out across the pillow like thousands of thin spider legs. Her skin was flaky. Jesus had seen this in almost every case of demonic possession. The human body, especially the fragile bodies of children, was not meant to house entities such as demons. Wrapped tightly in Adina's thin arms was a doll made from linen and straw.

A smile spread across her lips, forcing her cheeks to puff out. "I didn't think you would come, Son of God." The voice that came from the child was that of a gentle girl's with a voice much darker and contaminated projecting it outward. "This poor soul should mean nothing to you. Certainly, *your* God doesn't need it."

Karam let out a soft gasp and left the room in a hurry. Hearing her daughter speak like this caused her great pain, and she hoped that God knew these were not the words of her daughter.

"Our Heavenly Father loves each and every person on His earth, demon. You may believe you can convince us otherwise. You may think yourself strong. Your strength compares not to His," Jesus replied. He stood firm, showing no signs of fear and kept perfect composure.

Judas stood behind him calmly, bearing the cocky expression of a man who'd already won. He tossed a date in the air, catching the chewy dried fruit in his mouth.

The demonic laugh shook the walls, causing chunks of dried mud to fall from the ceiling. The wind picked up outside and blew the sand hard into the side of the house, forcing some through the shuttered window. The salty smell in the air was replaced with the putrid smell of vomit and dead fish.

Still using the innocent voice of the little girl, the demon said, "Your—Heavenly—Father . . . cares for no man. No woman. No child. Drop your petty allegiance to *Him*, and I will give you the true power to heal. You can be what he will not allow you to be. *You* can be a GOD!" The temperature in the room increased considerably as the demon spoke, like a slowly dying fire had been stocked back to roaring life.

"I want nothing other than what my father, the one true God, gives me. He knows what is best for all of His children. Now demon, I am growing tired of you. You will release the child Adina." Jesus stepped closer to the bed and looked directly down at the girl. The peacefully calm expression on her face remained. In a commanding voice Jesus spoke, "Demon, you will leave this child at once. Withdraw your foul taint from her body."

Adina began to convulse violently. Jesus could see her pale skin crawl as if hundreds of beetles scurried beneath it. Foam and blood seeped from her mouth, and her eyes opened at last to reveal the glossy dark red orbs they had become. She gasped for breath through clenched teeth. The demon within her let out a scream that shook the room with enough force to send cracks spider-webbing up the mud walls and across the floors.

Judas stepped close to Jesus and prepared to protect his companion from whatever perils may present themselves. He placed his right hand protectively on Jesus' chest as he stood to the left of him. While Jesus kept his focus on the girl and the demon that tried to take her soul, Judas watched for debris falling from the ceiling or any objects the demon may propel at them.

As quickly as it all started, it ended. The girl lay peacefully on her bed clutching her doll. The blankets were disheveled around her and her right foot was now uncovered. Jesus slid the blanket up slightly to reveal the scars and bruises the demon caused from being in her fragile body. The girl's skin looked to be aged well beyond her years. The encounter had taken its toll on Adina, but Jesus knew his Father would heal this child.

"Jesus. It is not over," Judas spoke softly. Despite the increased temperature, their breath was visible in the air. Neither man looked worried, yet a slight look of confusion showed on Jesus' face.

"You're powerful, Demon, but you're not as strong as God. You're not welcome in this home. I will only ask you politely once more to leave this child's body before I force you to leave."

Judas tossed another date in his mouth and bit down. The loud crunch caught him off guard, but before he could spit the date out he felt the handful of dates in his left hand begin to move. Half a dozen beetles crawled around in his palm where the dates used to be. Judas let out a yell and tossed the beetles to the floor in the corner before spitting out the crushed remains on the beetle he'd bitten into.

The demon began to laugh once again. "I AM MORE POWERFUL THAN YOUR GOD!" The demon was irritated, and Jesus could sense the anger. "You wish for me to remove the taint infesting this child's body?"

Black sweat seeped from Adina's tanned skin. It gave off the smell of sewage. Jesus had never seen this before, and he found himself wondering what kind of foul monster could produce such vileness. Within seconds it was retracted back into her body.

Adina's soft voice said, "Or I can drown her in it." The black liquid bubbled up from her mouth and ran from her nose. It streamed lightly down her face and soaked into her bedding.

With the desire to end this as quickly as possible, Judas began to chant a prayer as he pulled a small clay bottle from a leather satchel he wore at his side. He walked toward the bed, and with each step he took the bed shook harder. He had accompanied Jesus on many exorcisms, and knew that he must not show fear; however, he hasn't seen many demons hold their ground after being commanded by the Son of God to leave. There were, of course, a few who could, and he knew that none of them should be taken lightly. Mind wandering, Judas was taken back to the demon they faced in Joppa. So much chaos.

The bed stopped shaking as the girl said, "Please don't hurt me, sir. I don't want to die." Adina looked up at Judas through her large brown eyes—glistening with tears—as he lowered the bottle closer to her. "Please make it stop.

I'm so scared," she pleaded. "Bethesda will protect me." Adina held her doll tight against her chest.

Confused, Judas looked back to Jesus who, despite his own confusion, wasn't ready to let his guard down. They both expected the demon to attempt to trick them, after all, they'd seen it before, yet they were unable to tell if Adina managed to fight for a moment's worth of time or if this was nothing more than a cruel ploy.

"We will allow no harm to befall on you, this day or any other, Adina," Judas spoke as he turned back to the child. He looked down into her brown eyes just as they rolled back into her head. The demonic red flooded in like spilled wine. A worm breached the right eye, wriggling several inches of its body out before retracted back inside.

Raising the clay bottle, Judas poured its contents out over the child. Instead of splashing against the grinning face, the cool water was flung against the wall as if carried by a great breath of wind. Neither of the men had seen this before, especially with water that was blessed by the word of God, and both grew irate over the demon's amusement with the girl's plight as the laughter shook the walls once again.

"Release the child at once, demon. This is your last opportunity to do so. Any further attempts to challenge my authority, or my patience, will not end in your favor," Jesus said in a commanding tone.

"Does the Son of God grow angry?" the demon asked with a mocking tone that no longer included the girl's voice. "Perhaps you see now that you are weak, along with your God. I will destroy this child and then I will destroy you." The demon dragged *you* out for several moments longer than necessary, the voice growing deeper as it did.

Judas' anger rose and he reached forward to grab Adina. His hands collided painfully with an unseen barrier, bending his fingers backward and forcing hideous pops from several knuckles. In the same moment, he was propelled across the room, colliding with the wall. He fought to remain conscious while his head cleared and the pain in his hands subsided.

The demon laughed harder, causing more debris to fall

from the ceiling and walls as they quaked. "This child is mine. Now please." The shaking stopped as the demon's voice quieted to a gentle whisper. "Leave us in peace, and I will spare your souls."

Jesus stepped forward and placed his left hand confidently on Adina's brow. The barrier was either gone or couldn't stop the Son of God. "I will pray for you, demon—I forgive you for the evil you have wrought upon this child," Jesus said with sincerity.

Jesus raised his hand off of the child and stretched his arm out above his head as if reaching for the heavens. Judas, knowing what he was required to do, grabbed Jesus by the wrist, and the two men looked briefly into each other's eyes. With one quick motion, Judas pulled a dagger from his belt and ran the blade across Jesus' open palm.

With blood trickling from his open left hand, Jesus placed it on Adina's doll. "Bethesda will protect you," he said. In a powerful voice, he spoke in a language so ancient even he wasn't sure what it was. It was a language that hadn't been spoken since God created the earth, and he could feel that his body had become a conduit for a great power.

These words had never been spoken by Jesus, and he was startled to hear them coming from his lips. These were certainly not the words he'd intended to speak nor were they words he'd even known. Somehow he felt as if something within the room was drawing them out of him. The demon perhaps? Could this be some demonic treachery?

The shrieks erupted from the demon within Adina as the true word of God fractured its essence. Blood pooled on the girl's face between her eyes and nose. Jesus tried to stop as he listened to her bones break, but the powerful force he had unleashed was too strong for him to contain. Blood began to spray from her nose, and her hair turned gray and became dry and brittle.

Calm settled in as Jesus stopped speaking, and the demon's cries faded away. He looked down at the lifeless body of Adina. Her skin had become dehydrated and wrinkled as if she'd aged a hundred years. The blood on her face and blankets was already brown and coagulating. He dropped to his knees and laid his head on her bloody bed as he began to sob.

Judas placed a hand on his friend's shoulder. "We must go, Jesus. The child is dead, but her soul still needs to be saved."

Jesus lifted his head and turned to him, Adina's blood was smeared across his face like war paint spreading from his right cheek to his left. He looked at Judas and saw blood dripping from his ears. He knew whatever power he unleashed here could have killed them all, and he wished that such power would be removed from him and this world. Those thoughts were quickly silenced, and without contemplating what Judas meant, Jesus felt the girl's soul somewhere nearby.

In his left hand was the doll Adina had been holding tightly. It was covered in blood, only some of it his own. The doll's onyx eyes peered lifeless from the now red face. Adina's soul radiated from the doll, but so did something much darker.

"We need to hurry. She is trapped with the demon. You are right, Judas. We must save this child's soul and destroy the demon." Jesus stood with the help of his friend. "Thank you for standing by my side once again. You are a true friend, Judas."

Judas smiled at Jesus and looked one last time around the small room. The wind had died down, and the sun's rays penetrated the shutters. The battle had caused the house to shift enough to knock down a slab of the dried mud and boards that made up the ceiling, blocking the doorway. The two men pushed hard, but the blockage would not budge. For several minutes they tried, hoping Adina's mother would be able to pry it open from the other side, but she never answered their calls.

"I guess we go out the window," Judas suggested. He forced the shutters open, and the warmth hit his face. Both of them looked away as they waited for their eyes to adjust to the bright light of the sun.

After helping each other climb through the window, they stood yet again in the hot sand. Jesus could not believe what he was seeing. The home had collapsed. Everything but the child's room was now a pile of clumpy sand, leaves, and wood. The barn that Judas put their camels in had also been destroyed. Their bodies lay in the sand, shredded, flies already feasting on the gut piles.

"KARAM!" Jesus yelled as he ran around the wreckage. "Karam!" He continued to cry out for her as he started digging in hopes of finding the woman alive. "Karam." This time it came out as a sigh as he found her.

She lay under a patch of straw and palm leaves just at the edge of the wreckage that was once her home. Her head had been smashed by the large wooden support beam. Chunks of her brain were stuck to everything close by. It took them fifteen minutes to remove her body, and two hours to dig a grave in the soft sand.

They had no idea how long they were in the girl's room. It seemed like only minutes, but the early morning sun was rising in the east, and it was well beyond midday when they first arrived at Karam and Adina's home. The warm wind crept gently through the desert, creating a liquid effect as the loose sand was brushed along.

Jesus prayed for the woman's soul. She was in God's hands now, but the feeling that he failed her here on earth could not be shaken. Finding a way to save Adina's soul so she can have eternal life by her mother's side would be his priority, even if the pursuit of this goal killed him.

I

June 7th, 8:09 P.M:

Roughly seven miles north of Muscatine, Iowa, off of Highway 38, is the small town of Kathrine, with a population of four hundred on the dot, according to the last census. It was a quiet little place where neighbors knew each other well, kids still played in the streets, and the smells of a single summer's BBQ could water mouths in every large, grassy yard from one end of town to the other. Being such a small town, there were only homes, with the exception of a small gas station that sat just on the outskirts along the highway.

In this small town of Kathrine sat a small white two-story house at the end of its short paved driveway just off of Maple Street. It took up very little of the big yard it sat on and didn't compare at all to the larger houses around it. The yard was well maintained, but the exterior of the house was rough, also not comparing well to the houses around it. A new coat of paint on the wood siding would go a long way, but more than anything it was in need of a complete renovation.

A modest yet large church sat directly across the street from this house. It stood in the center of the small Iowa town. The big cross that stood off the top of the steeple was lit brightly, radiating magnificently through the night sky. It could be seen for a mile, and it welcomed lost travelers. Not the travelers driving past Kathrine from Muscatine to Wilton (or vice versa) down Highway 38, but those that traversed life, doing the best they could to be the gracious souls the Good Lord desired His children to be.

"Did you put your shoes by the door, Tim?" asked Edwin Carmichael, owner of the little white house on Maple. After his divorce, he tried to calm down a bit, but even in the calm voice he spoke in there could be heard the anger that festered in his brain. After all, it was his temper that drove his wife away, drove her to find a new lover and eventual husband.

Edwin was just slightly shorter than average height. His short brown hair was often messy regardless of his desire to have most things neat and orderly, and his blue eyes stood out under his thin eyebrows. A bad temper and plenty of stress caused wrinkles to form on his forehead despite his last birthday putting him at just thirty.

Edwin's ex-wife, Karen, whom he left last year, took everything he had worked so hard for. The five-bedroom house *he* bought so they would have room for *her* family. The three car garage so *her* family could park in it when they came to visit. There was no way in hell their car would sit out in the sun; it would be too hot when they went to leave. And when it rained or snowed, no way in hell, it would rust (pay no attention to the rusted rocker panels the late eighties BMW already sported). And when it was just plain gloomy outside, no way in hell . . . for whatever reason.

And to top it all off, Karen left the kid with him. No way in hell did he want his son living with him. It wasn't that he didn't love his son, but he knew he wasn't the best person to take care of him.

All of Edwin's money that hadn't gone to Karen's family went to her friends. For a stay-at-home mom, she sure did spend his money well. The second he walked in the door from work she left to go out with her girlfriends. Edwin didn't mind much at first, as he knew having friends was important, but it was important for him, too. He never saw his friends. Hell, most of his friends had given up on him entirely.

Karen would take her girlfriends out to dinner, out to the movies, and out to the spa on an almost daily basis. After years of being madly in love with the woman, there was only one way Edwin could describe her.

Bitch!

And that was putting it as nicely as he could.

His six figure income certainly made them in the top of the wealthier group of where they lived, but he had nothing of his own to show for it. Trying to figure out how she took everything from him in the divorce when he was given Timothy was too much for his mind to wrap around successfully. He had to give credit to her lawyers for a job well done. More than anything, he was just thrilled to be keeping most of his income (despite Karen trying to take all of that, as well), so he chose to rent the house they lived in until he could build up a nice sum of money to sit happily in his bank account.

"No Dad," Timothy answered, knowing quite well that his father could see that his shoes were not by the door, and the question was more of a reminder than an actual question. The five-year-old boy pulled his shoes off of his little feet without even undoing the Velcro straps and tossed them by the door from where he sat on the couch.

"Dammit, Timothy!" Rage brought Edwin's blood to an instant boil. He stood tall over the boy and looked into his blue eyes. He knew those were his own baby blues looking back at him, and this managed to quell his anger just a bit, but only just a bit. "What did I say about being lazy? Are we lazy, Tim?"

"No, Dad," Timothy said, holding back tears. He feared his father like no child should have to, but he believed that his father would never really hurt him intentionally.

"Up the stairs, now!" Edwin barked out the order like a drill sergeant. His voice wasn't exactly deep, but it felt heavy in the air when he was angry.

With the intentions of building his son up into a strong, successful man, Edwin made a quick exercise for situations like this. Anytime Timothy showed any signs of laziness or weakness, Edwin would march him to the top of the stairs and back. This was Edwin's idea of a brief lesson in doing what you're told or working harder than needed. It wasn't much, but both he and Timothy knew it could be worse.

Timothy knew better than to show any signs of anger, despite his father being an almost constant sign of anger. He stood up straight and walked to the bottom of the stairs. Without missing a beat, he stepped up on the first step and kept going with Edwin close behind. The little boy's light brown hair was just long enough to bounce with each step. His soft feet made almost no noise on the hardwood steps.

The light was off on the second floor, and even though the boy was afraid of the dark, he knew better than to use that as an excuse to not stand on the top step. After all, successful people strive for the top, regardless the obstacles that stand before them. His father had told him that many times. Timothy turned back toward his father as he reached the top of the landing. Edwin stood at the bottom, watching with crossed arms and a smile on his face that didn't really seem all that happy.

"That was more work than taking your shoes to the door, wasn't it?" Edwin asked.

"Yes, Dad. It smells bad up here," Timothy complained. His nose crinkled before he pinched it shut with the thumb and index finger of his left hand.

"It does not. Stop your crap and come on back down." Edwin's patience wore thin quickly despite his numerous attempts to control his anger.

"Seriously, Dad, it smells awful." Timothy unplugged his nose long enough to catch a whiff of the air around him then quickly plugged it again.

"You probably spilled your milk up there. Dammit, I told you not to bring food and drinks up here." Edwin stomped up the steps in a hurry, each heavy footfall echoed in the narrow stairwell, never taking his gaze off the small boy. His sights were set on his son like a hawk dive-bombing a mouse in a field.

"I didn't have milk u—" The boy's sentence was cut short as his shoulder was grabbed by a long arm that extending quickly from his bedroom door. Black as coal, long, thin, and marked with a few scrapes and cuts, the arm was joined by a second. The hand on the second arm gripped Timothy's thin neck. At first, the arms appeared to be nothing more than quickly stretching shadows, drawn delicately by the light of a car that had just turned to corner onto Maple, but as quick as the arms appeared Timothy was pulled into the bedroom to his left. Into the blackness that cloaked the second story of their modest home.

"TIM!" Edwin howled in terror as he launched up the stairs, taking the last few in one jump. He turned quickly to his left and ran into Tim's bedroom. The smell at the top of the stairs was of used motor oil with a mix of burnt flesh and rotting meat. He turned on the light and immediately dropped to his knees as a sharp pain exploded in the bottom of his foot.

"FUCK!" He screamed as he picked the Ninja Turtle action figure up off the floor and threw it into the corner of the room. Thanks to the adrenaline that pumped vigorously through his body like nitrous through the engine of a drag car, the pain was brief, and while still on his knees, Edwin looked around, examining every inch of the large room. There was no sign of his son.

Throwing himself onto his stomach, he lifted the bed skirting and looked underneath. A few toys, a shirt, and a teal Captain Planet cup from Edwin's own childhood were all that was under there.

"I knew it, you brat!" Rage began to build back up.

The pain began to throb in his foot again and escaped his mouth. He pulled the cup from underneath the bed, gripping it tight enough to turn his knuckles a chalky white. Sticky milk residue clung to the inside of the cup, but only the most subtle odor was beginning to waft from the spoiled milk.

"Where are you hiding, huh? I'm going to beat your ass when I find you!"

Edwin continued searching the room for Timothy. He came to the conclusion that the arms he saw pull his boy away must have been his eyes, and those delicately drawn shadows, playing tricks on him. Timothy just darted into his room quickly. After checking the closet, Edwin looked under the dresser. There was plenty of room under there for Timothy to hide, as Edwin discovered one day after the boy refused to finish his supper.

That particular incident was hard on Edwin. Spurring him to buy an anger management CD he listened to on his drives to and from work. He lost control that day, and instead of a swat on the butt, Edwin clenched his hand into a fist and struck Timothy twice in the back. To make that even worse, Edwin piled the food high on Timothy's plate. He knew when he did it that there was no way the boy would be able to finish it all. He was angry, and he couldn't help that, but too often he saw the monster he must appear to be to his son. Too often he felt that he created reasons to be angry with his son.

After regulating his breathing and slowing it down to normal, he began to count out loud: "One . . . Two . . ." The counting wasn't a threat aimed toward Timothy. "Four . . . Five . . ." Instead, it was to give him time to regain control of himself. Edwin didn't want to be angry. He hated being like that, but he didn't have much control over it. Instead of having an Anger Knob that could be slowly adjusted, he had a switch. It wasn't like a light switch, however. A light switch couldn't contain the level of anger that could be pumped through it. He needs a four hundred amp safety switch, something out of Frankenstein. And that switch didn't take much to flip.

"Timothy?" Edwin called. "Where are you hiding, buddy? I'm calm now." Even he could hear in his voice that that wasn't quite true. "You can come out. I'm not mad about the milk. I just want us to go back downstairs and we can turn on Adventure Time before bed. How's that sound?"

He stood in the center of the room waiting. He knew there was nowhere else for him to look, and he couldn't help but be impressed by Timothy's hide-and-seek skills with as well-developed as they were. Edwin kept carefully watching for the boy so he knew where his new hiding spot was. Total silence enveloped the man, and he strained to hear even the faintest of noises. His controlled breathing sounded like an airplane taking flight. Edwin heard nothing other than that, not even the soft whimpering of the scared boy, and he felt his temper flaring back up. It took everything he had to keep it in check.

"Timothy!" Edwin called once more. He could hear the anger roll off his tongue and tried to hide it. "Come out, please. I'm not going to wait all day. If you don't come out soon I'm going to shut the lights off and head back downstairs. You'll be all alone up here in the dark."

There was nothing but silence for the next five seconds that was broken by a wooden rattle from behind Edwin. It was the kind of sound heard in TV shows when a young couple moves into a small apartment next to the train tracks and their cupboards clatter every time the train flies by.

Spinning quickly, Edwin stared hard enough at the dresser to strain his eyes. His ears perked up. Waiting for the sound that he knew would return. Taking two steps toward the dresser, he held his breath to eliminate the noise he was making.

A second rattle escaped the dresser. This time, Edwin saw the middle drawer quiver as if it were a fearful animal caught in a hunter's trap.

Taking another slow step forward, he realized there was no need for sneaking. There wasn't anywhere for Timothy to go from there.

The drawer rattled again.

This time, it shook the entire dresser hard enough to rattle the change in Timothy's piggy bank. Edwin lunged forward. In the moment just before grabbing the brass handle he felt as if he'd just walked into the grocery store on a hot day. Cold unexpectedly surrounded him, sending a chill that hit his bones like taking a punch from a professional boxer. Ignoring the sensation, Edwin grabbed the handle and pulled the drawer open in one move.

Staring back at him was not the face of his son, but the face of a dark skull with empty eye sockets that saw everything. The skeletal face emerged from between the rows of Timothy's jeans. It was chalky and smokey but firm in appearance. It looked like oily water inside a glass skull, smooth and perfect and impossibly eerie. The face lifted several inches out of the drawer, and the bare teeth, transparent yet defined, clicked together.

Another wave of cold engulfed Edwin, only this time it originated from inside of his body. Ice crystals formed in his lungs, and his blood began to freeze in his veins. A brief moment of horror fired in Edwin's brain as he imagined his veins bursting open like frozen water lines. Before Edwin could scream, the face was pulled away.

His bottom jaw hung loose for several seconds as he felt the unusual feeling of his insides thawing. "What the fuck?" he finally managed to say. Edwin hadn't realized how far backward he'd jumped, but he crept forward five or six feet before he could look down into the drawer. It was empty of everything that was not the little boy's jeans. His heart was pounding, but he let out a laugh from deep in his gut.

"It was just a shadow from a car driving down the street," he reasoned weakly, momentarily forgetting about his search for Timothy.

And then a thud came from the bathroom across the hall. Edwin stood in place and listened. The unidentifiable smell of oil grew thick once more. He continued to listen for the next sound, but he was also becoming concerned about where the smell was coming from. There was nothing up here but Timothy's room, a spare room he used as storage, and the bathroom. His car was due for an oil change, but he didn't change his own oil anyway, so Timothy wouldn't have anywhere to get oil from.

When the silence continued, Edwin began to look around for the smell. Moving around methodically, he determined that the smell was consistent in every spot of the room. It was just as strong in the closet as it was under the bed. Chasing the smell was maddening but enough to take his mind off of his earlier scare.

"Help, Dad!" Timothy's voice drifted in eerily from the bathroom. It was slightly muffled, and something about it gave Edwin goosebumps that rippled over his flesh like cheering fans doing the wave at a football game.

Forgetting the odor, Edwin crossed the hall in one step and flipped on the bathroom light. He stopped immediately and called out for his son, "Timothy? Daddy's here, big guy. Where are you?" He was terrified and didn't know why. Anger had completely vanished, but fear bombarded him from all sides. Something about a child calling for help would put any father on edge.

He immediately bounded toward the vanity and pulled open the doors under the sink. There was nothing but a few bottles of cleaner and extra rolls of toilet paper. Edwin stood, turned to the bathtub, and pulled the curtain over so hard that the rod fell from the wall and clanged sharply on the tile floor. The tub was empty, and Edwin had no idea where to look next. The bathroom wasn't any bigger than a closet. In frustration, he dropped to his knees and wiped the tears away as they rolled down his cheek.

The sound coming from behind Edwin made him stand up as if he were a private whose drill sergeant walked in unannounced. It was a sound that Edwin would describe as Timothy smearing his wet fingers on the window in the back of the car (which he would have yelled about for several miles). In this case, Timothy must have been smearing up the mirror. Edwin smiled for only a second as he felt relief in finding his son, but then his anger swelled up inside of him. His senses, still telling him to be afraid, were silenced by the overwhelming rage.

"You like playing tricks, you little brat?" Edwin spun around quickly to grab Timothy off the sink. Instead, he looked through the empty space above the sink and into the mirror; Timothy's eyes were red from crying. Pure terror dominated his face. The boy screamed and pleaded, but Edwin couldn't hear any of the sounds he made. He tried desperately to break free of the mirror. The boy's little fists hit the glass but the only sound to come through was a muffled thud.

"Tim! Timothy!" Edwin yelled as he pounded on the mirror. He cried harder as the horror of what he was seeing set in. "I'll get you, son." Edwin drew his arm back and prepared to punch through the mirror.

Before he could, however, a dark figure appeared behind Timothy. The black, skeletal face he'd seen in the dresser drawer once again looked right through him into his soul with those empty eye sockets. The teeth seemed to fade in and out of existence as the grotesque mouth opened wide. The smoke that made up the skull was as black as charcoal and rolled around much quicker than it had when Edwin first saw it in the dresser.

"Bring me back my boy!" screamed Edwin. He pounded on the mirror firmly. "Please. Give him back." The tears flowed down his face as he pleaded with the dark figure. He never realized how much he loved Timothy until this very moment, and it wouldn't set in until much later that he can't remember the last time he'd told his son that. Right now he would give his life and soul for that chance.

He leaned close to the mirror to take a good look at his son. There was so much terror in the little boy's eyes that Edwin could feel his heart shatter in his chest. With the first tear to hit the sink, the dark figure in the mirror hissed laughter, a sound that came out like an angry cat fighting a snake. The lights flickered and the mirror vibrated. The figure wrapped its bony black fingers around Timothy's face.

"Don't touch my son!" Edwin ordered. "I love you, Timothy. I'll get you back." He slammed his fist into the mirror, causing cracks to spider web out from the center to each corner. The figure hissed once again and began to back away with Timothy.

Moldy green lines crawled up Timothy's face toward his eyes, leaving the flesh around the lines seared. He could hear the terrible creature's laughter but not his son's cries, and without realizing it, he was relieved by that. Hearing the fear and pain in his son's screams would certainly kill him right there on the spot, yet he felt a new strength surge in him, and Edwin's fist collided with the mirror a second time. Broken slivers of mirror and chunks of drywall rained down onto the vanity and floor.

Edwin stood frozen in place as he looked at the cracked drywall behind the mirror. His son was gone, but he wasn't ready to accept that. He beat on the drywall until it too no longer hung from the wall. White dust suspended in the air like fog and stuck to Edwin's teary face as he looked into the empty space of the interior wall.

He found it funny how the wall was as empty as he felt, but he was not finished fighting for his son. "I'll get you back," he said, staring into the empty wall. "I'll get you back, and whatever *you* are . . . I'm going to fucking crush you."

II

June 7th, 9 A.M:

The birds sang in the morning sun on that beautiful day in that quiet Iowa town of Kathrine; it was a day that gave no warning that it would end in a terrible tragedy for a father and son. Laughter filled the air as children played in yards of freshly cut grass while their parents raked the remaining clippings into piles. Piles that, as soon as the parent's backs were turned, the children would plop into with a run and a big leap, scattering grass clippings for several feet.

The Church of Christ sat magnificently on its corner lot with Maple Street to the north and Cherry to the west. It stood out like a giant among the houses that surrounded it. The Sunday service hadn't started yet, but the church-goers were already piling in, hoping for a chance at their preferred spots. Older folks tended to sit closer to the front so they could hear and see better, while younger folks stayed closer to the back. The kids specifically sat as far back as possible so they could play with their toys and phones without being bothered by their parents.

As the first people to arrive filled the church, two men talked in the basement surrounded by the sounds of muffled conversations and the soft thuds of footsteps above them. Pastor Simmons, a tall man with gray hair and a shaved face, was dressed for today's sermon. Raised in a Christian family, Pastor Simmons was nothing less than a true believer in the word of God. He lived every aspect of what he taught. Waiving the large home the church owned for him to live in, Pastor Simmons chose to live in a much smaller house around the corner.

His entire life was devoted to serving God, so he had no children, and he never married. He talked the church board into renting the large house to a homeless family. With his assistance, they were able to turn their lives around with educations and new careers. The house has been empty for three weeks, as the once homeless family moved on in hopes of the house being used to help another family in need.

“The recent storms have caused enough flooding to fill a lake,” Pastor Simmons said. “There have certainly been an unusual number of them the past few weeks. Not much water got in here, but there is mold. My nose may be as old as I am, but it works well enough that I can smell the mildew when I come down here, and you can see the foundation may need a bit of a face lift. Kind of like myself.” He chuckled pleasantly. His face was kind yet craggy. Marked with deep wrinkles that may very well have been caused by the years of smiling this pleasant man had done.

“It will take me a few days to come up with a solid estimate, but as soon as you approve it I’d like to get started,” Lincoln Scott said as he looked over his notes. He wasn’t as tall as the pastor. His long brown goatee hung down below his sternum, and his brown eyes, set perfectly in his handsome face, gave off a sense of warmth and caring.

“Absolutely. Are you going to be joining us this morning?”

Lincoln always found it hard to follow along with religion. He respected everyone’s beliefs, but he didn’t share most of them. “I—I’m sorry, but I haven’t been to church since I was just a little kid. I’d like to think I’m a good person, but I have too many questions that can’t be answered by God.” He felt his well-chiseled jaw clench after the words left his mouth, as he assumed the pastor would tell him to take a hike. Only followers of the good Lord can work in here, but Lincoln was surprised by the pastor’s reply.

“Relax,” the pastor said, noticing the man’s immediate concern and respecting his honesty. “I’m not going to fire you for your beliefs. Remember, you don’t have to believe in God, you don’t have to follow him, but he believes in you, and he will follow you everywhere you go.” The hand the pastor placed on Lincoln’s shoulder was rough from years of the hard work the older man enjoyed as part of his service to the Lord.

Lincoln replayed the words a few times in his mind but didn't say anything.

"You can start working whenever you like. Today even. Please don't make too much noise until after everyone leaves, though." He continued on before Lincoln could say anything, "Oh, there is some cracking in the wall over here," and he led the speechless Lincoln to the center of the basement. "It's strange that this only started cracking within the past few days. This part of the basement has always remained dry, and overall the wall has always been solid."

"I appreciate you wanting me to start so soon," Lincoln said, finding the words to speak, "but I don't even have an estimate made up yet." Lincoln was excited to have the pastor's confidence, yet he would rather wait until they had all the details. "It will take a few days to figure up how much time it will take and what supplies I'll need to do the job."

"I don't need your estimate. You're an honest man. I know, because you were raised by your grandmother. She was an honest woman, I can see in your face you're just like her," the pastor replied. "Just send me the bill when you're finished. Don't forget the receipts! The church loves receipts. Heaven help me if you don't send those with the bill."

"Thank you," Lincoln said sincerely. He turned from the man and examined the cracking bricks and mortar. The wall was actually a four foot square pillar in the center of the basement. "Yeah that is pretty bad. I'll put some jacks under here and replace all of these bricks. This pillar seems to be here for support. It shouldn't be too much extra work, but it will definitely increase the cost."

He wanted to take those last words back as soon as they left his mouth, sucking the words back in with a deep breath before they reached the pastor's ears. Pastor Simmons has done so much for him. Although Lincoln had never quite found God, his grandmother had been in this church every Sunday for over sixty years. When she passed away, Lincoln couldn't afford to bury her. Pastor Simmons donated the money and put together an amazing service.

Even after Lincoln could easily afford to repay what was spent, Pastor Simmons refused. Lincoln had this debt in mind now as he thought about his estimate on a job he was now comfortably going to take a loss on.

"You charge what you must, Lincoln. I know that your price will be more fair then anyone else's. And don't try to repay a debt you don't owe," the pastor added as if reading Lincoln's mind. He patted Lincoln on the shoulder once more and handed him a key. "That will get you in through the back entrance. It's just over there." He pointed past the cracked brick pillar and toward a door that led out of the basement.

"Thanks, I'll return it when I'm done," Lincoln said. He pulled his own key ring out of his pocket and ran the church key through the loop while his other keys jingled in his palm.

"No, thank you. Feel free to come and go as you please until the job is finished." Pastor Simmons turned and walked across the basement and climbed the stairs. While walking away, the pastor said, "I do expect everything to be done in a timely manner, however, but I trust you'll prove up to the task."

An hour later, Lincoln found himself sitting on the top step, staring down into the basement. He had listened to the entire sermon. Much of it didn't make sense to him. It was all just random stories on being a good person and the sacrifices Jesus made, and that is how he remembered it from his childhood. There were no answers. There were no solutions to his problems, yet he felt good, and he guessed that is why people came here.

From the corner of his eye he caught a brief glimpse of a figure moving quickly through the shadows along the far wall of the basement. The soft patter suggested it was someone small and barefoot. If it was a child, they stayed just out of reach of the lights, but he could still hear their footsteps padding around in the dark. Lincoln stood and walked down the stairs. Reaching out, he flipped the light switch that lit the other half of the basement. They hadn't used those lights earlier, as all the work he needed to do was on this side, so he wasn't entirely sure if the lights over there even worked.

The bright fluorescents came on with a soft buzz that Lincoln could hear from across the basement, but all that accomplished was illuminated the other half of an almost empty room. He could make out a large stack of plastic storage totes and nothing else.

Hello?" he called out. "I'm sorry, but you can't be down here. There's mold and some bricks that might fall." He walked around the large basement. "You need to go back upstairs with your parents. I'll be starting some construction down here and I'd really hate to see you get hurt."

There was nothing but silence as Lincoln walked around in search of the kid. When he approached the cracked brick pillar in the center of the room he noticed that there was a black liquid dripping from one of the cracks in the seemingly ancient mortar. It looked like used motor oil, yet it was as thin as water when he ran his index finger through it.

It only dripped out for a moment before stopping. Lincoln, out of curiosity, sniffed the thin liquid that was on his finger. The thin oil had a very strong salty odor that made the bridge of his nose crinkle. He had never seen anything like it and didn't have much time to think about it as the silhouette of the child flashed quickly in the corner of his eye once again. He snapped around on the heel of his right foot, certain that he had caught the unsupervised child. Instead, he was startled by the man standing behind him.

"You haven't started yet?" Pastor Simmons asked with a warm smile.

"I uh, I listened to your sermon," Lincoln replied. He wasn't sure why admitting this to the pastor made him feel uncomfortable.

"I know. I thought that was you. Besides, I'm only kidding with you. Start whenever you're ready, but please don't hold off too long. I'd hate for this place to fall down on us." Another pleasant smile deeply wrinkled his already furrowed face.

Lincoln returned the smile before saying, "I'll get

started today. I was actually going to start with this pillar. By the way, there was a kid down here playing around. I was trying to find him—or her, for that matter—and have them get back upstairs." Lincoln was hoping that the pastor would say he saw the child run up, yet the man quickly changed the subject.

"Do you have anybody working with you, an assistant perhaps?" Pastor Simmons asked. "I could probably find a few guys willing to help out."

"On big jobs I bring in my nephew. I'll get started on my own first. It helps keep costs down if I can do most of the work on my own. If I run into issues, I just give him a quick buzz and he is on the jobsite in thirty minutes or less," Lincoln responded.

"Sounds like a good kid, must be a hard worker like you."

"Yeah. He's sixteen, likes to make extra money for clothes and spending running around town with his buddies. He's always willing to work for a few bucks."

"Well, I have some things to attend to. Please stay safe down here, and if you need help, please seek it. I don't want to have you break your back because you thought you could do something on your own that you can't." There was genuine concern on the pastor's face.

"I know. Thanks," Lincoln said with a smile.

"I'm serious," Pastor Simmons said in a stern voice, a playful grin crossed his lips. "I know that you picked up your grandmother's strongest quality, her stubbornness."

Without another word, the pastor walked back up the stairs. His voice trailed down as he spoke to the departing churchgoers. Lincoln turned back to the pillar in the center of the room. The black liquid was gone, and there was no trace of it on his fingers. Another minute past before Lincoln shook it off as his eyes playing tricks on him.

He walked out through the rear door. The sunlight was so bright he had to squint to see anything as he waited for his eyes to adjust. Avoiding the traffic created by all the people leaving the church, Lincoln pulled out of the parking lot in his beat up Chevy pickup. The late '70s truck was a rusty blue, but the big block 409 was well maintained under the hood.

The engine came out of his father's '62 Impala. His father was killed in that car during a car cruise hosted by a local club. He tried to show up some young punk that thought his was tough in his daddy's Mustang, couldn't stop at the red light, and was hit by a semi. All that was salvageable from the car was the engine. Lincoln polished it up, replaced what needed replaced, and dropped the powerful engine into his grandfather's pickup. He didn't need all the power his father cranked out of it, so he cut it back to a more practical four-hundred and thirty horse power and gained some gas mileage. He did, however, keep the dual four-barrel carburetors perched atop the high-rise aluminum intake.

Every time he climbed into that truck he knew he would start working on the body someday. He told himself that all the time, but the money was never there for this particular project. He had a hot rod in the garage at home and his house itself was still a work in progress. But so much of his time was spent cruising that old truck around in the summer that his left arm was always much tanner then his right.

Lincoln watched the small town roll by as he drove through it. There was something about small towns that made him feel at peace. He spent some time in the larger cities a few hours away. Des Moines, Chicago, and even St. Louis, but none of these places were home. Life moved too fast in the city, and Lincoln just wanted to cruise at a comfortable pace.

The blue Chevy rumbled like a purring beast as Lincoln backed up to the rear church door an hour later. In the bed of his truck were four adjustable floor jacks, each capable of supporting twenty-thousand pounds. He certainly didn't plan on lifting the church, but they would be more than enough to take pressure off the center pillar while he made the necessary repairs.

Once he had the jacks securely in place, he began carefully removing the bricks. He stacked them neatly several feet away. When he had the opening in the brick pillar down far enough to see in, Lincoln was shocked to see that it was completely hollow. He was certain that with the layout of the basement and the size of the building that this would have been a major support of some kind. With nothing inside, however, he knew it couldn't be. Although he had studied the layout of the large basement numerous times, he peered around once more, amazed at how large this room was, and how there seemed to be nothing supporting the floor above. It would bring the cost up, but he couldn't leave this job without placing a proper support down here.

Lincoln decided to come back to this in the morning when he could bring in everything he'd need and continued with his work elsewhere. A playfully sinister smile spread wide across his face as AC/DC's "Highway to Hell" began to play on the small radio he brought with him. "What a perfect song to listen to while working in the basement of a church," he said aloud.

Something kept drawing his attention to the pillar, and he chalked it up to safety concerns. He pried several more rows of bricks from the structure and looked once more into a shallow hole inside. Enough light cut through the dust particles that he could just make out the shape of a small, dusty box sitting all alone in the dirt. Lincoln reached down and lifted the box out. It was made of smooth wood and roughly the size of a shoe box, and he could see gold markings as he brushed the dust away with his hand. The markings turned out to be a symbol etched into the wood and filled in with gold. He assumed it must have been a holy symbol. It was of a circle with a cross inside. Touching the bottom of the circle was the top of a five-pointed star. At the center of the star was a black stone.

Lincoln slid the latch to the side and the lid opened on its own as if it were spring loaded. The temperature in the basement dropped considerably, sending a shiver through Lincoln's skin, and although the lights remained on (buzzing ever so softly), it grew quite dark, as if the light was being sucked away by a vacuum. Every time Lincoln exhaled, his breath escaped in a thick cloud. A slight breeze ruffled his shirt and blew through his long goatee. The moving air was warm, made to feel hotter by the cold air that surrounded him.

He shook out the chill and glanced inside the box. Lying peacefully at the bottom was a little doll that he decided must have been ancient. The arms and legs were made of straw, and it was wearing a faded, dusty dress made of linen. The linen had become brittle, and cracked when Lincoln picked it up from the box. He quickly set it back down to avoid damaging it further, but he couldn't close the box. There was no latch or lever that he could see to free the hinges of their locked position.

"Bethesda!" The voice came from directly behind Lincoln, and it caused him to jump. A little brown haired girl stood behind him. She wore a filthy linen dress that looked as if it was made from the same bolt of linen that the doll's dress was. "I've been looking for her for so long." She sounded surprised to see her doll again, as if she had just about given up hope.

"Who are you?" Lincoln asked. His heart was still racing, but he didn't want to show it. "You shouldn't be in here. There is remodeling going on. Something could fall on you, or there could be asbestos." He knew from the inspection that there wasn't asbestos (that had been cleared out years ago), but he hoped it would keep her and any other neighborhood kids out.

Her attention snapped from the doll to Lincoln. The girl's eyes rolled back in her head, revealing bloodshot whites that seemed to have yellowed with age like centuries old paper. She let out a high pitched scream that caused Lincoln to drop the box and the doll. A brick fell from higher up in the pillar, smacking him on the top of his head just inside his hair line. Both hands went to his head as he fell to his knees. Blood ran down his face, and a large drop built up on his nose before falling, landing on the doll and soaking quickly into the parched material. The lid snapped shut around the doll so hard it caused dust to puff up around the box.

The little girl's screams made it hard to keep pressure on his head where the brick had hit. To save his eardrums he moved his hand down and covered his ears, but that did nothing to quiet the scream. It was coming from inside his head. A noise so sharp it felt like it pierced his brain. Thousands of needles jabbed into the back of his eyes. Eventually the pain and noise overcame him, and the world around him went black and quiet. Thankfully it went quiet.

III

June 7th, 9:12 P.M:

The quiet spring night in the small Iowa town was shattered by dozens of flashing lights. Six police cruisers, one ambulance, and even a small fire truck were parked in front of the two-story white house. Reds and blues painted the exterior of the white house in a dance that created vibrant pinks and purples. A bit of overkill, but this sleepy little town, and the ones surrounding it, never saw much action. The occasional DUI, traffic stop, and the rare bike theft were about it. There wasn't a kidnapping in over a decade. Despite the presence of so many emergency vehicles, the town was dead quiet.

The magnificent light show drew people in like moths to a flame. Everyone on that side of the town was either on their lawn or leaning out an open window. Several teenagers had their cell phones out capturing the scene on video to be uploaded to the internet as soon as the juicy details were released. Residents that were not fortunate enough to live nearby were on their *routine-late-night-walk* that just so happened to take them right past the action.

"What do you think happened?" an older woman with a wrinkled face and white hair asked another woman.

"I bet that man murdered his family," the reply came from the lady standing inside her open window just two houses up the street from Edwin's house. She was pulling the curlers out of her freshly dyed hair and preparing to put on her best outfit. She knew it would be an all-out race to the news van, and she knew she had to look her best to get on TV. "I heard yelling coming from there just a few hours ago. I never saw the wife much, but I could tell the husband was abusive. He was always yelling and throwing things." This was said as much to the gathering crowd as it was in rehearsal for her seconds in the spotlight.

"I hope he rots in hell," said the first old woman without the need for any actual proof of what was really going on.

Inside the home, Officer Alex Martinez stood in the living room next to his partner, Officer Cory Stevens. Officer Martinez stood just under five feet six inches tall. His short dark hair was thinning in the back. A thin mustache darkened the area above his upper lip. He looked down at the distraught man who was sitting on the couch in front of the two officers. Reading facial expressions was something he was trained for. Eye movement, micro-expressions, but he couldn't nail down a solid read on the man.

Officer Stevens was taller than his partner by a full six inches. His face was clean shaved, and his blond hair was kept short, a habit from over a decade spent as a military police officer in the Army. A career path he'd chosen to follow in his early twenties. There was an honesty that could be seen in his green eyes, but there was also a stern nature about them, and as soft as they looked, they penetrated everything they looked at, seeing well beyond just what they saw on the surface of things. Overall, Officer Cory Stevens gave off the impression of a man who cared for people but wouldn't take shit from anyone.

Edwin looked up at both of them wondering why they weren't springing into action to find his son. Through his tears, however, he could see that the officers thought he was insane. Both officers stared down at him in disbelief of the story he just told them. Edwin knew their minds were working at full speed trying to sort through the information he'd given them. Neither one would believe that this man's son had been pulled through the mirror by a dark figure. Not for a second. He should've known better and told less of what he saw, but that would have felt like a lie, and lies are always found out.

Officer Stevens took notes in his brown leather-bound notepad as Edwin talked while Martinez tried to make sense of the situation.

"Sir, I'm not saying that we don't believe you. We have officers out looking for your son as we speak. I know this is a very tough time for you, but you have to trust that we are doing everything we can right now," Martinez said.

Part of him wanted to comfort a father who had lost his son, while the other part knew to remain as professional as possible. "The description you gave us is of a middle-aged black woman, correct?"

"What? No! It *was* black. Pitch black like your boots. Besides, I can't say for sure if it was a woman or a man. The body was grotesquely thin like a skeleton," Edwin said as the frustration built, knowing full well that he was just as much to blame as anybody. After all, he didn't have much solid information, and he knew it, but this wasn't the time to let that Anger Switch get flipped to its pissed off position, so he tried desperately to stay as rational and calm as possible.

"Your story doesn't make sense, Mr. Carmichael. People don't get pulled through mirrors and disappear into the wall, and I've never seen anyone with skin that's literally black as you describe it," Stevens argued as his No-Bullshit attitude took over. His eyes squinted slightly—a micro-expression he didn't notice—as he tried to figure out this man before him and what his gain would be from the loss of his son. Several thin wrinkles broke the otherwise smooth forehead that filled the space between his hairline and thin eyebrows. For a man who'd seen war and death he'd certainly aged well.

"That's exactly what I saw. I don't know what more I can tell you!" Edwin raised his voice as he spoke. He struggled to keep a mental finger on that Anger Switch in his brain and hold it in the calm position. Standing up he continued, "I didn't hurt my boy. I know that's what you think and I get it, but as crazy as it sounds, he was pulled through the mirror by a *black,* skeletal figure."

Stevens placed his right hand over his sidearm in a motion that wasn't intended to be subtle as he held back a cocky smirk. Respect was beaten into him in the military and engrained in him by his father before that, but something about Edwin and his story rubbed the veteran the wrong way. "Sir, you just need to sit back down and relax. Like Officer Martinez said, we have officers out looking for them. Is there a chance that in your frightened state you mistook the bathroom window as the mirror? It seems more likely—now I'm not saying you're lying—that he was taken out through the window. *Or* perhaps you saw the reflection in the mirror."

That one had almost convinced him, but he knew what he saw and said, "No, he was taken through the mirror. He was *inside* the mirror." As soon as the words left his lips he regretted it. That could have been his way out of his crazy sounding story.

"Did you see him being pulled through?" Martinez asked. He felt the look his partner had given him for asking such an absurd question. Of course the man didn't see his son being pulled through, Stevens would later say. At which point Martinez would bring up the fact that the more questions they asked, the more answers they would get, to which Stevens couldn't argue.

"No. He was already in the mirror when I found him. I tried to get him out, but the mirror busted and there was nothing behind it."

"So you don't believe there was a chance you just saw the reflection?" Stevens asked, giving Edwin an unconvinced look despite trying to play nice again.

"No, he wasn't *IN* the window. He was *IN* the mirror." Edwin could feel his face turning red. He was logical enough to understand how this sounded, but he also knew what he saw. Crazy or not, he was going to find his son.

"Let me go over your son's description once more to be sure I have it written down correctly. He's five years old, light brown hair, blue eyes. Last seen wearing a white t-shirt and tan shorts?" Martinez read back from his notepad.

Edwin nodded that this was correct.

"How about you try to get some rest, Mr. Carmichael? I know it won't be an easy night for you, but please try. That's the best way you can help us right now, and the best way to help your son is to keep your strength up. We'll keep a watch on the house in case your son returns or any suspicious people come by. There will be patrols out all night looking for him," Martinez said calmly.

"Why the hell did I even call you? You don't seem to understand! Some *thing* took my boy!" Edwin stepped toward the officers.

"I've had enough of your crazy shit!" Stevens roared. He slammed Edwin down onto the floor and rolled him over onto his stomach. It happened so fast, and Stevens had such an unbelievable control over Edwin's body, that the terrified father never had the chance to even think of struggling before he was in handcuffs.

"What are you doing?" cried Edwin. "You can't arrest me for wanting to find my son."

"You're not under arrest, yet; however, you did just assault a police officer, so I am taking you for a little ride," Stevens said with a morbid pleasure in his voice. The other officers that were searching the house all stopped to watch.

"No. I have to find my son. Please let me go so I can find my boy!" Edwin began to fight as the much stronger man pushed him through the front door and out into the yard. Although it was dark outside, the flashing lights from the remaining police cruisers and the ambulance lit up the yard. "I didn't do anything! I didn't do anything!" he screamed as he was shoved into the back of one of the cruisers.

"What are you doing, Cory? Neither of us knows anything other than his son is missing. If my son was missing I'd be upset, too." Martinez didn't believe Edwin's story either, but he couldn't imagine what he was going through.

Officer Stevens didn't say a word. He just looked at his partner. He served in the Army from the time he was twenty-three. There were crazy people in this world that would do anything, no matter how crazy it sounded, and Stevens knew this all too well.

He had a flashback of a seven year old boy in Afghanistan. Stevens sat on the hood of a Humvee writing a letter home to his parents. The small boy walked up to a group of six soldiers who were standing around the guard post right outside of their base. "Can I have some water, please?" the boy asked courteously.

"Sure thing, kid. What's your name?" Stevens heard one of the soldiers ask as he handed his canteen to the little boy.

"Thank you for the water," the boy said without answering the question. He took several large drinks, handed the canteen back to the soldier and said, "God bless America." In that very instant the bomb under his shirt detonated. The blast tore the boy's fragile body apart and knocked Stevens off the truck. Although the soldiers remained intact, none of them survived.

Stevens knew that it was a father who had sent that little boy out to die that day. That chicken shit probably spared his own life by doing so. That brutal memory is as vivid now as it was when it happened. Because of that, Stevens decided he would never trust the word of any parent until he had the facts. In his eyes, Edwin was guilty of murder until proven innocent.

"Fry that bastard!" the old woman in her window shouted as the group of women watched the police officers load Edwin into the back of a black and white.

"Serves him right," another woman exclaimed after waiting for her bladder to finish emptying into her adult diaper. She quickly said her goodbyes and walked away before the piss smell became noticeable.

The Channel 6 News van turned onto the street as the car transporting Edwin turned out. The old woman in the window, despite her eyesight getting bad when it suited her needs, spotted it immediately. Perfect timing, too, as she had just finished putting in her best earrings. She grabbed her jacket, checked herself one last time in the mirror, and, feeling satisfied that she would look better than anyone else at this hour, ran out to flag down the news crew to tell them how devastating this whole ordeal was for her.

June 8th, 12:02 A.M:

Edwin sat in a small holding cell at the police station just a minute's drive north of Muscatine. He hadn't been scared like this since he was a child watching his first horror movie. He couldn't quite put his finger on what scared him more: being in a jail cell after seeing his son kidnapped, or losing his son to some horrifying creature in the mirror. The latter was beginning to sound more like one of those horror movies, and he began to experience lapses of doubt. Perhaps this was all a dream. Maybe he was going mad.

Maybe I have a brain tumor. That would explain a lot. My anger issues, this vision of a creature taking my son. Maybe he had gotten scared when my sanity disintegrated, ran outside and was hiding under the porch. Maybe I'm not in a holding cell. Instead, this is my new room in the looney bin.

No, he was sure of what he saw. He had always been rational-minded, albeit quite angry. There has always been an explanation; maybe he did just see the reflection through the mirror. Then he realized that the only window in that bathroom is a small octagon with stained glass. It was only a foot in diameter. There's no way anyone could go in or out of it, especially with a scared child fighting them the entire time.

But at least the guards at the jail house took care of him. They brought him a sandwich and a soda. One guard talked to him as if they were old friends, even if he did take all of Edwin's stuff and placed it in a plastic bag when he was first dragged inside. At least he got to keep his clothes. He had no interest in being dressed like an inmate. He was also glad he didn't have a mug shot taken. Officer Stevens had calmed down on the drive over and decided not to arrest him for assaulting an officer. Instead he was just being brought in *for further questioning*.

Even though he was terrified, Edwin was drifting in and out of sleep. More a side effect of what his mind had witnessed than a symptom of being tired, he was sure. He didn't want to sleep, though. He wanted to stay awake until someone brought his boy back. Yet he knew he couldn't be any help from this cell. He patted the metal bench and thought, *they could've at least put me somewhere with a cot,* and laid down on his back. He wasn't sure exactly what time it was, but it had to be around midnight. His eyes closed and he slept.

June 8th, 2:17 A.M:

"Daddy," Timothy said. His timid voice sounded both near and far. The source was close, but the sound travelled an unimaginable distance to reach Edwin's ears.

Edwin heard the voice squeeze through the layer of sleep he was cocooned in and felt relief flood his mind. *It had all been a dream!* He opened his heavy eyes and couldn't wait to wrap his arms around his son. *What a horrible dream!* For a moment he felt like Ebenezer Scrooge waking up on Christmas morning a changed, and much happier, human being. But as the sleep-haze cleared he looked into the dim light of the holding cell and his heart dropped. He felt the warm tears build up in the corner of his eyes.

He sat up and listened, hoping that Timothy would call out to him again. Hoping the police—officers Martinez and Stevens—would walk into the holding room with his boy looking shaken up but otherwise alright. But he heard nothing. There were no sounds at all. He walked to the bars and peered around the corner. He could see through a window that it was too early for the sun to come out, but he couldn't quite see the clock. It was hard for him to imagine that everyone had gone on break at the same time, leaving the place completely unattended.

"Daddy." Timothy's voice came from directly behind him but again sounded distant. It wasn't a whisper. It was weak, as if it had taken up most of its power to reach him.

Edwin felt the hairs on his neck stand and the goosebumps form mountain ranges across his flesh. There was something he didn't like about his son's voice. He released his grip on the bars, a grip he didn't even know until than that he had, and turned slowly.

The face he looked into was that of his son, but the eyes belonged to someone else, some *thing* else. Smoke rolled around hypnotically between the little boy's eyelids. There was also a hint of something red burning in the center of each one like a tiny ember fighting to erupt into existence as a brilliant flame. Timothy's body was suspended in the air several feet from the ground, putting him at eye level with his father. Blood trickled from his ears, and his guts were strung out across the floor like a plate of spaghetti that had been knocked from the table by a child.

"What have you done to my boy?" Edwin screamed. Even his voice came out weakened as if the strength was pulled out by the air around him. He tried to lunge for his son, but his legs failed him. There was a brief feeling of the floor falling away from him before he dropped hard to his knees. He would later discover that he may as well have been slammed down into that kneeling position on his knees, as he was left with tender, dark purple bruises.

"Pray for him," Timothy said in a voice that wasn't quite his. He let out a demonic laugh, and his guts, spread out on the floor, squirmed as if they were joining in on an inside joke.

"Stop it! Please!" Edwin's plea sounded hollow as he cried out. "Just let my boy go. Let me have him back." He broke out in heavy sobs. "Surely a creature such as you has no need for a little boy." *Did I really just try to reason with it?*

"Little Timothy is much safer with me," Timothy said. "I won't hurt him. Not . . . at . . . all." Timothy smiled so wide that the soft flesh making up the corners of his lips tore slightly. Blood dripped from the torn skin. "Ok you got me. I lied, but his soul is just the beginning. You should be proud. Your little boy is numero uno in my book. He's my first, and you never, ever, forget your first."

Timothy—the monster controlling his body—shrugged playfully and the red embers in those smoky black eyes flared up brightly. "Ok, you caught me again. I just can't pull the ol' wool over your eyes." This beast's attempt at humor infuriated Edwin, whose blood was running hot as it was. "He may not be my first, but this one's special. I need the power that was encased in that fragile little body. So fragile."

A thick black tongue fell from Timothy's mouth. It hung down so far Edwin thought it would fall right out of his son's head, but it quickly retracted before the creature continued talking. "It gave me the power I require. You see, I have a little opposition in my quest. There are some who don't approve of what I'm doing, but they can't stop me now. I will continue to feast on Timothy's soul. His spirit, his fighting spirit, is so . . . fucking . . . delicious."

The walls around them shook vigorously as the beast inside Edwin's son grew more intense, and a rush of disbelief overwhelmed Edwin. He felt like a mouse being toyed with by a cat. "Whatever you need, you can take it from me. Just give him back, you fucking monster!" He tried to move, but he felt as if his knees had been glued to the floor, and the flesh would be ripped from his kneecaps if he stood.

"He's mine now." Timothy said cheerfully in his own voice. "Can't you see that? Can't you see your little boy's dead body? There are his guts, spilled out on the floor. They fester before your eyes. The insects mate in his intestines. Their offspring grow in his stomach. He doesn't get another chance at life either way. He's dead either way you slice it." Timothy's face lit up humorously, and the sickening smile spread. "Kind of like the way I *sliced* open his belly."

"I'm going to fucking rip you apart you piece of shit! I'm going to fucking murder y—"

"What are you screaming about, Edwin!" Officer Stevens barked from the other side of the bars.

"My boy—Timothy." But when Edwin looked back toward where his son had hung in the air, there was nothing.

"Alright, man. I think you need some serious help. I'll call . . . what the fuck is that?" Stevens looked past the kneeling man to the pool of blood on the floor where Timothy had been just moments earlier. He opened the cell and walked in to take a closer look. "Did you do that? Is that yours?"

"Yeah," Edwin replied. "I spilled my *fucking* blood all over the place."

Officer Stevens, who would have otherwise busted someone in the mouth for talking to him in that tone, accepted that he deserved that one. The two men stood above the puddle and watched as maggots, centipedes, and worms crawled and wiggled, enjoying themselves in the sticky pool.

June 8th, 8:13 A.M:

"That's not possible," said Martinez after hearing the story from both Edwin and Stevens. A man who quite often believed in all things spiritual and most of the unexplained, Martinez was rational enough to know that now wasn't the time to feed into what Edwin was experiencing. "Mr. Carmichael, I'm sure you just had a horrible dream stirred up by the traumatic event you've suffered. The blood was probably just rusty water leaking from somewhere in the ceiling. I've already put in a work order to have the city maintenance guys come check it out. It probably looked more like blood because the lights are dimmer back in the holding cell."

They had moved from the holding cell to the guard's break room. The janitor pitched one hell of a fit when he saw the mess, and Stevens grew tired of listening to him bitch about it, but they were closer to the coffee machine, and all three of them could use as much caffeine as their bodies could get.

"It wasn't a dream," Edwin argued. "Some creature took my son." He was surprised to find out that it was almost eight in the morning when Stevens had come in to the station to finally punch out and heard him yelling like a lunatic. He usually worked the afternoon shift, but pulled an all-nighter to help search for Edwin's son. Several guards were working all through the night and had made their rounds, but none of them heard or seen any of this.

Edwin had trouble dealing with the fact that he wasn't sleeping but appeared to have lost several hours. Anything that lent credibility to the opposition was frustrating at this point.

"Obviously I'm not buying this creature story, but I know blood when I see it, Martinez." Stevens stated, sounding a little irritated that his judgement would even be questioned.

"Hey, I meant no offense. You have to admit, it seems like a crazy place for blood to be found when nobody in the area was bleeding." Martinez said in his defense, a defense that frustrated Edwin even more, as it was nearly infallible.

Stevens nodded, understanding perfectly well where his partner was coming from.

"I'll drive you home, Edwin," Martinez said after an uncomfortably long silence. "We didn't arrest you, and we have no other reason to hold you here." He turned to his partner. "Go home and get some rest, Cory. We'll sort this out this afternoon."

"Yeah, I could use some rest," Stevens stated and shook his partners hand before giving Edwin a surprisingly pleasant nod.

After putting away some paperwork, Martinez walked Edwin out to the cruiser. "You can sit up front. We really aren't supposed to let people, but with what you've been through I think you deserve a ride-along."

"Thanks," Edwin said. He appreciated the man's kindness, but he still had to force a smile.

"So do you believe in ghosts?" Martinez asked as they climbed into the cruiser.

Edwin felt blindsided by the question but answered it anyway. "No. That's ridiculous." Even he could hear how unconvincing he sounded, so he continued, "I mean, I guess it's a possibility, you know."

"You say you saw a black figure, possibly a woman, take your son through the mirror." Martinez didn't want to upset him, but he wanted to try and better understand the man.

"Yeah . . . yeah I guess I must believe in ghosts, or boogeymen, or demons. Whatever the hell that thing is."

"I'm really sorry, Edwin. I want to get to the bottom of this as much as you do."

"Do you believe me?" Edwin asked; he hoped the man would say no. Saying yes would mean that more than one of them may be crazy.

After a long exhale that sounded like a gradually deflating tire, Martinez answered, "I think so. You know those movements we see out of the corner of our eyes, those chills we get at random or the feeling of being watched? It's been proven that our bodies have an incredibly high level of awareness that our minds will never be able to accept. You may think I'm crazy for saying this." He caught the daring look Edwin gave him. "Ok, maybe you won't. My grandmother passed away when I was twelve. I continued to talk to her until I was fifteen. I didn't just go to her grave; she came to me. We would talk for hours at a time. When she finally stopped, I thought it was just a way for me to cope with her lose, but there has always been that feeling that she truly was there with me."

"I really want to say that sounds crazy. A few days ago I would have. But after what's happened—what I believe has happened—I'm really not sure what to think anymore." Edwin looked out the passenger's side window, hoping that their conversation, at least this conversation, was over. There wasn't much scenery this time of year. Corn was starting to grow, but other than that it was all open fields as they drove back to the little town of Kathrine, and Edwin's home.

Edwin could see the yellow police tape around his house as they pulled onto Maple Street. Several "power-walkers" trudged on past without taking their eyes off the place, probably not the first time today, either. *Looky-loos. Get a life you pathetic shitstains.* He hated that, especially the assholes that would stop in front of him on the highway to get a better look at an accident when it was on the other side of the damn street.

When they realized it was him, their eyes went front-and-center, and their power-walk proved to have some power to it, after all. He knew as soon as they rounded the corner by the church they would be on their phones and the phone tree would be a go. All hands on deck. Everyone in town would know that he's home before he can step through the door. But he didn't care because they were nobodies, anyway. He just wanted his son back. Timothy was all that mattered.

Finding out that he still had a job would be a plus.

He thanked Martinez for the ride and took the officer's card so he could call if he had any more information, or if he just needed to talk. Walking into his house was disorienting, most of his effects had been moved during the search that took place after he'd been so generously asked to vacate. The officers who were so careful with his things while he was there must have left after he was escorted out, only to be replaced by uncaring assholes.

He gave his boss a call and was relieved to hear that all was good. To his employer, he was in great standings, and at least they would honor innocent until proven guilty. He could return to work when he was ready. Maybe, just maybe, he would take the whole week off.

IV

June 8th, 3:28 A.M:

Lincoln's house was an older two-story craftsman style home that he bought at a foreclosure auction right before he married Kaydence. It sat on just over five acres of land, most of which he leased out for farmland, putting a nice amount of money into a college fund for his daughter. His property was in the middle of nowhere with Kathrine being the closest town to him two miles to the east. He liked how secluded it was, being the only house in the middle of hundreds of acres of farmland had a calming effect on him. Very little traffic and no neighbors was exactly how he felt it should be.

Tonight he tossed and turned in bed. Despite how tired he was, he couldn't fall asleep. He had a strange feeling in his gut, like something was terribly wrong; not with him, just in general. He had woken up in the basement of the church after what he figured was an hour long nap. Fuzzy memories of finding a doll and a little girl playing down there bounced around in his head like a ricocheting bullet. But neither were anywhere to be found when he woke up. It must've been some mold that got to him. He'll have to remember to wear a mask tomorrow and make mold removal a high priority.

Despite his nap, he'd gotten home around six, showered, ate supper, and spent an hour on the couch with two lovely ladies: his wife, Kaydence, and their seven year old daughter, Sadie Elizabeth. Their daughter had her mother's jet black hair and hazel eyes. Although Kaydence kept her hair slightly above shoulder length, Sadie liked hers long so it could be braided.

After Sadie went to bed, Lincoln cracked open a cold beer and Kaydence poured a glass of wine. They made love with half their drinks warming on the nightstand. Kaydence fell asleep quickly after, but Lincoln started his tossing and turning, praying to any god that would listen that he didn't wake up Kaydence or she'd surely put him to sleep the hard way; the way that had him waking up with a black eye.

He lay on his back, listening to his soft heartbeat and the gentle breathing of his wife. His eyes slowly drifted around the dark room, gliding smoothing but never really focusing on anything in particular. Just enough light shone in from the hall light for him to make out the silhouette of everything in the room. It was almost early enough to call it quits and stay awake, but he hated going to a job with no sleep. He could have pulled that shit five years ago, but not anymore.

Counting sheep is something that had never worked for him before, but he gave it a try. He imagined them jumping in from the hallway, landing quietly on the hardwood floor of his room despite their hooved feet. At least they better land quietly or they'd wake Kaydence, and if they did that, well, Lincoln knew he'd be put to sleep the hard way. From there they would jump onto the dresser, then jump to the other end of it. Never walking, always they'd jump.

The first sheep—completely invisible, of course, as his imagination didn't quite run like it used to—jumped from the edge of the dresser and arched over the chair in the corner and bounded over the dark figure sitting patiently in it. The second sheep, also invisible, prepared to jump when Lincoln realized what he had just seen.

His eyes snapped back to the chair, and his heart rate skyrocketed. The dark figure continued to sit comfortably in the chair, unmoving. Lincoln watched it, trying to focus on it, trying to determine what exactly it was. It looked like no jacket he had ever placed on the back of a chair. And neither Lincoln nor Kaydence owned a hat other than their winter stocking caps, and unless she starched the hell out them there was no way a stocking cap could stand like that. Whatever it was, it was perfectly motionless, nothing more than a picture. He shuffled through his mental photo albums for every hanging-clothes-closet-monster he had ever been afraid of as a kid, but none of them looked this vivid.

After several long moments of staring directly at the shadow figure, Lincoln decided that's all it was: a shadow cast from several different objects in his room mingling with a tree outside that just happened to overlap perfectly. It was a longshot of a theory, but it was the best one he had. That, however, didn't explain how this picture-perfect collection of shadows was staring back at him almost as hard as he was staring at it.

He found himself hoping that a car would drive by. The headlights would slice through the shadowy form to reveal it wasn't really there. This hope was shattered by the realization that he not only lived on a nearly deserted road, but he lived too far off that road for this to happen if someone was to drive past.

Staring at this shadow was making his eyes sore, but he couldn't look away. It stared right back at him in a way that made his skin crawl as if it would slither right off his body. Lincoln refused to let this get in his head, but he felt that it wanted in his head. This shadow was just that, a shadow, and certainly not looking at him. He waited for this thing to move, knowing how silly he must look locked in a staring contest with something that wasn't even there.

Regulating his breathing and forcing his muscles to relax was more work than he would have imagined it would be. There was just something in the air that had his senses on high alert. It had been several more minutes before Lincoln decided he'd lie down and wipe this from his mind. In the morning he'd take whatever the hell was in that chair and toss it out, no exceptions.

Dropping his head back down to his pillow, Lincoln stared up at the ceiling. Now his eyes wouldn't close, and the room was either slowly rotating around him or his eyes were drawn to the shadow figure in the chair. Either way he couldn't look away. There was no fighting the fact that his mind had to know what this thing was before it could rest easy.

For Christ's sake, you're a grown man, Lincoln!

Finally he sat back up and reached down to flip the blanket off his body. He was too old to cower under the covers.

Then the shadowy figure stood up in one quick, choppy motion like a man walking past a strobe light. There was a subtle creaking sound that Lincoln heard but couldn't determine if it came from the chair or this dark intruder's joints. A deep smell of motor oil brought back a memory he didn't have time to place. In the same moment this figure stood it had already taken two steps toward the bed. Its long thin arms seemed to flicker in the air as if they were having trouble staying visible in a world they didn't belong in.

Lincoln jumped up in a way he would never be able to explain, somehow going from sitting on his ass to his knees without the use of his hands. The scream that escaped his throat was dry and deep. Kaydence sat up, eyes wide open, heart in her throat, and she was also screaming.

"What is it, Lincoln?" she said as she stared at him, allowing her eyes to dart around the room quickly before locking back on him. Her heart beat a mile a minute, as did his. He didn't answer, only looked straight ahead into the corner of the room. "Babe, what's wrong?" she asked again, this time giving him a gentle shake before sitting up on her knees and wrapping her arms around him.

He pulled away just enough to look into her face. Even distorted with the fear she felt, he thought she looked beautiful. It took his mind a moment to clear before he realized he must've been sleeping after all, and what he saw was nothing more than a nightmare creature. It was gone now, but he still felt like something wasn't right.

"I'm alright," he finally managed. "Just a bad dream is all." His heartbeat began to slow, and he lay back down with his arm around his wife comfortingly, as he tried to hear down the hall hoping he hadn't woken up Sadie. His sleep was once again restless, turning to look at the chair in the corner every few minutes. Lincoln was pretty sure he was awake when he saw what he did, but he refused to believe it.

June 8th, 7:00 A.M:

The alarm clock on Lincoln's phone buzzed excitedly as the sun began to peek through the window, its warm rays stretching toward the bed, ready to warm all who needed it. Lincoln fumbled around before finally finding his phone and swiping across the screen to silence the blaring alarm. Sitting up, he looked once more at the chair, now well lit. The blue upholstery complimented the dull yellow walls perfectly. The yellow was a color Kaydence had picked out a few years ago that he was sure would look awful but turned out to be quite soothing.

He tossed the thick blanket to the side and quickly pulled it back. It was surprisingly cold. The AC hadn't been on in a few days, or at least he thought. Maybe Sadie turned it down playing with it. He just hoped that it hadn't killed the damn unit. He really didn't want to replace it.

The carpet was the first thing to go when they bought the house, and now he regretted it as his feet made contact with the freezing floor with each step. It was much colder as he walked out into the hall where the cold radiated off the walls. He felt nothing from the vent in the hallway as he walked by and was amazed that he could see his breath. Taking the stairs two at a time, he rounded the banister at the bottom and checked the thermostat. The switch was in the off position, and even if it had been on, it was set for seventy degrees. The current temperature read forty-one.

Lincoln shook the chill off his body and walked back up the stairs. The bathroom wasn't any better, he was glad he only had to piss, as the toilet seat would have been too cold to sit on. He laughed at the thought of how Kaydence would react. He expected she would hover. Warm air rushed in when he opened the bathroom window. It was only a sixty degree morning, but it was much warmer than in the house. He decided to open up the rest of the windows before waking the girls.

"Good morning, handsome," Kaydence said as she came downstairs. She was fully dressed and ready for the day. She hated the thought of wearing her pajamas more than she had to. "Does it feel cold in here?"

Lincoln sat in the breakfast nook off the kitchen, drinking a cup of coffee from the new coffee maker Kaydence picked up. It was one of the single cup ones that took the little plastic cups and poured its blisteringly hot water through them and into the mug below. He had her cup already made and sitting at the spot across from him.

"Yeah it was weird. I woke up this morning and it was so damn cold in here I could barely walk across the floor. Got all the windows open to warm it up. I really don't want to be the guy that has the heat on in June, ya know?"

"Yeah," Kaydence laughed. "I checked on Sadie, her room was still pretty cold."

"Really? Her windows were the second windows I opened after the bathroom. By the way, how cold was the seat?" Lincoln gave her that smile that made her fall in love with him the day they met.

"Fuck you," she said. "It was so cold I had to hover."

This spurred a good laugh from Lincoln before he was hit by a flying English muffin.

"You said you opened Sadie's windows? I guess I just realized that I opened them, too, just before coming down," Kaydence said.

"I made sure to open them," Lincoln said, almost defensively. "I'd hate for her to catch a cold."

Kaydence caught his tone and said, "I don't mean to say you didn't, I believe you. Maybe the windows slid back down is all I'm saying."

Lincoln shook his head slightly in agreement and said, "Well I'm heading up to wake her now, so I'll take a look at them." He downed the last of his coffee, stood up, and walked around the table to slide Kaydence's chair in for her as she sat down to her cup of coffee and buttered English muffin.

He walked up the stairs; the wood flooring was still cold under his bare feet. He had put his jeans on, along with a shirt, but decided the socks could wait. Now he regretted that decision as much as ripping out the carpet. The door to Sadie's room was closed as he approached, which was odd because he knew he left it open, and he was sure Kaydence would have, as well.

"Must've been a draft," he suggested, thinking out loud. "Sadie, honey, are you awake yet?" He wrapped his fingers around the doorknob and immediately drew them back in surprise; the brass knob was so cold he thought he'd grabbed a ball of ice. He reached again, quickly turning the knob and let go as the door opened. The windows, one straight ahead of the door and the other on the north wall to the right, were both shut.

The mist from his breath was so thick it lowered his visibility until it drifted above eye level. The little black haired girl lay on top of a pink blanket covered in cartoon princesses. Her nightgown smoothed perfectly over her small body. In her right arm, snuggled close to her chest, was a strange little doll. Lincoln didn't recognize the doll at first, but as he rushed in to cover her up his memories came back to him.

"Oh God," he said as he tucked her back under the blanket. He grabbed the doll and quickly opened the windows up once again.

The little girl coughed weakly, and Lincoln forgot about the doll, letting it drop to the floor in the center of the room. It landed face up on a pink rug that matched the princess blanket, sheets, and curtains.

"Are you alright, honey?" Lincoln asked as he placed his hand on her forehead. She didn't feel warm, but he wanted to be sure. "Wait right here. Daddy's going to run and grab the thermometer." He ran down the hall to the bathroom and opened the medicine cabinet, grabbed the thermometer and clipped a plastic filter over the probe.

As he walked out into the hall, he held back the urge to scream in frustration. The bedroom door was closed. He jogged down the hallway and grabbed the still cold knob. He turned it, but it didn't unlatch. Instead, it spun freely as if the latch assembly inside was missing. Lincoln pushed on the door, but it didn't move.

"Sadie? Are you alright in there?" he asked before placing his ear to the door. "Did you lock the door, Sadie? This isn't funny." He tapped his knuckles on the door loudly three times.

"What's the matter?" Kaydence's voice behind him caused him to jump. He found himself surprised that, with as on-edge as he'd been, he hadn't shit himself.

"I can't get Sadie's door to open," he said before quickly adding, "but don't worry. I was just in there and she's fine."

Kaydence jumped toward the door in a panic and grabbed ahold of the knob. Lincoln watched her, waiting for her reaction to the freezing brass, but she didn't seem to mind. In fact, she turned the knob and the door opened. Sadie stood in the center of her room and smiled as her parents came in.

"Are my waffles done?" she asked as her little arms curled around her mother's hips.

"Are you alright?" Kaydence asked. She hugged the little girl briefly before pulling back to examine her daughter. "The door wouldn't open. You weren't scared were you?"

"No, Momma, I just woke up and climbed out of bed. I was coming downstairs to get my waffles, with or without you guys." She had that dead serious tone that only an innocent child scalding her parents could produce.

"Ok, let's go, girly. I'll meet you down there." Kaydence patted Sadie on her bottom and watched her run from the room. "Don't run on the stairs!" she called after her. Turning to Lincoln, she asked, "Are you ok? You've been a little *off* this morning. That dream must have shaken you up quite a bit. What are you doing with the thermometer?" She pointed to his right hand as her train of thought was interrupted.

"Oh, I was going to check her temperature. You know, just to be proactive against this unexplainable cold spell. Anyway, I didn't think that nightmare bothered me, but it must be lingering around in my brain still. I'm sure getting to work will clear my head." He pulled her close and kissed her lips deeply. "Now you run along, but don't run on the stairs," he said as he smacked her ass.

She turned just long enough to give him a playful wink.

He stood in the center of Sadie's room for a few minutes. Looking around as if he'd misplaced something. He couldn't help but feel that that misplaced thing was his mind. The windows were open despite the fact that he was pretty sure that neither he nor his wife opened them. The warm breeze ruffled the pink curtains as it drifted steadily in. The feeling something was off continued to nag at him like a fly that kept landing on his ear. He forced the feeling to the back of his mind and walked downstairs, kissed his wife and daughter and walked out of the house.

June 8th, 7:52 A.M:

Pastor Simmons was outside doing some yardwork as Lincoln pulled off Maple Street and into the churchyard where the basement door was. He certainly had to admire the pastor's work ethic and dedication to his beliefs. This is something that the church normally hired gardeners to do, but Pastor Simmons insisted on doing it himself. Keeping the house of God looking good was as much a part of his job as tending His flock. Besides, he really didn't have much else to do during the week.

The sun was burning bright, and Lincoln more than welcomed its warmth. The chill from his cold house stuck to his bones like the time Sadie stuck chewing gum in her own hair to save it for after lunch. He just couldn't shake free of it. He smiled and gave Pastor Simmons a wave as he drove his pickup carefully through the churchyard and around to the back. The last thing he wanted to do now that he saw who maintained the grounds was tear up the grass.

"Good morning," Simmons said cheerfully as he walked toward Lincoln, who returned his greeting. "Listen, I guess I didn't think anything of it yesterday, but I want to thank you for coming in on a Sunday. Working on Sunday is what I do for a living, and I fear that it may have been inappropriate of me to have you come out yesterday. I hate that I pulled you away from your family, but I didn't realize that the situation was as bad as it was down there until I walked down to grab a box of candles. I may have overreacted by calling you in instead of waiting until this morning."

"Don't worry about it, Pastor. That's what I'm here for."

"Are you feeling alright, Lincoln? You look a little pale this morning," Pastor Simmons said, concerned.

"Yeah, just a rough night," Lincoln responded before adding, "There's nothing to be too alarmed about. I didn't get sick from anything in the basement. There is mold down there, as you pointed out, but I stayed pretty much away from it, and today I brought the gear I need to take care of it. I feel awful because I just renewed my mold removal certification, so it's a no-brainer that that is the first thing I *should've* done yesterday."

"I really would feel awful if something down there caused you any harm. Either way I'm glad to hear you're well on your way to getting us all squared away and safe. Well, back to my work I go. There's no rest for the faithful." Pastor Simmons chuckled vibrantly as if he'd told a joke and walked back around the church.

Lincoln pulled his keychain from his pocket and shuffled through the keys until he found the one given to him by the pastor for the basement. It took some wiggling for the key to fit into the lock, and then he found the basement door overall to be a little tricky, requiring some jiggling and turning before the lock came free. The wooden door required some strength to open, as the bottom of it dragged against the concrete floor and emitted a deep scratching sound with every inch it budged. Rusty hinges sang along with the wood-on-concrete scraping in their own annoying squeal until the door wouldn't open any further.

A bead of sweat ran down his forehead, catching in his right eyebrow. It wasn't until he wiped it away that he realized how much work it was to open the door. He even questioned why it was locked. Anyone breaking in would need a nap after that workout. Shrugging off the slight fatigue, he made a decision that he would take the door off and sand the bottom down later in the day. For now, he had something a bit more urgent to take care of.

His first job for the day would be to begin on mold removal; how this slipped his mind yesterday he didn't know. He carried a large roll of plastic to block off any openings leading out of the basement. After building himself into quarantine, he put on a white jumpsuit, plastic gloves, and a facemask that made him feel like a government scientist in a sci-fi flick (going perfectly with his quarantined room), grabbed a spray bottle full of water to reduce airborne spores, and made his way back to the basement. He dampened the mold spots and began scrapping the toxic fungus away, dropping the clumps into a bucket of bleach.

He decided to work through his lunch break. He had no interest in fighting his way out of this suit only to squirm into another later. It had taken him an entire nine hours to clear the place of all the mold. The stuff just seemed to keep popping up. By the time he was finished working, he was starving and drenched in sweat. He ripped his way out of the white suit, cleaned up in the restroom on the main floor, and made one last pass through the basement to be sure he had the area clean. He decided to leave the plastic up to deter any more kids from playing down there, even though he knew there wasn't anything going on except Wednesdays and Sundays.

Just as he reached the basement door, he heard his name whispered from across the room in a distant voice that was somehow soft like a child's and gravely like an old man who'd been smoking his entire life.

Lincoln spun, eyes shooting around the room as he looked for the source of the whisper. "Pastor Simmons?" he asked despite being pretty sure it wasn't. "Hello? Who's down here?" He walked slowly around the basement. The lights flickered softly but stayed lit. He could hear the sounds of someone breathing but couldn't determine where it was coming from. Briefly he thought it was the room around him breathing but realized that just didn't fit into the world he knew.

There was also an overwhelming smell of wet dog and motor oil that seemed to dig into his nose, making him gasp for fresh air while trying to shake the smell from his nostrils. The air had become sour and hard to breathe in, and for a moment he thought he would suffocate. He scurried around the brick pillar in the center of the basement and glared curiously at it. He hadn't forgotten about the black liquid that seeped from it, or the box with the doll.

The doll that was in Sadie's room!

He turned to run for the door but his foot caught something mid-stride. Reaching his hands out, he managed to break his fall as he rushed toward the hard floor. Light puffs of dust arose as his rushed breathing disrupted where it'd settled on the floor. His hands stung from the impact with the smooth concrete, but he was relieved that the pain was in his hands and not his head. Lifting himself up a few inches, he looked back and was shocked to see a small boy, curled up in the fetal position on the floor. His light brown hair was matted with blood. Lincoln couldn't tell if his shirt was white or red, looked like white with dark red splotches.

The boy moaned a little and lifted himself up with his dirty arms.

"Shit," Lincoln instantly felt bad, first of all for swearing in a church, second for swearing in front of a little boy. "Are you alright, kid? Are you hurt . . . lost?" Lincoln helped the boy off the ground.

The boy lifted his head and looked into Lincoln's eyes. Looked past them, really; he looked right into Lincoln's soul. The boy's eyes were gray with red splatters that seem to bob and weave as if they were living creatures trapped inside those gray globes. Blood soaked through what Lincoln finally felt confident to confirm was at one time a white shirt. Insects crawled over the boy's skin, which was pale and looked as if it would be cold to the touch. The boy shot to his feet in one quick move, but he didn't stop there. The little boy continued to rise up until he floated a foot off the floor.

Lincoln's paternal instincts said to grab the boy and get him to the nearest hospital. His survival instincts told him to get the fuck out of there. His brain went into overdrive, piecing together the scene his eyes relayed. None of it made sense, and the latter instincts won. Lincoln screamed, propelled himself backward and jumped to his feet. He bolted up the stairs and out the door into the bright afternoon. As he pulled his truck door open, he realized that he still had plastic and tools and buckets of mold that needed to be cleaned up properly. He fought with himself for just a moment before turning back and facing the stairs that led down to the open basement door. He hadn't locked it up, either. Leaving a jobsite looking like this could cost him this and future jobs.

The little boy stood in the doorway in a pile of guts up to his knees. He smiled up at Lincoln as the man came cautiously into view at the top of the stairs. The boy's cheeks were torn at the corner of his mouth, making his smile appear to be much wider. Blood trickled from his mouth and dripped out of his hair like an endless fountain.

"Fuck this," Lincoln said and turned to run.

"I'm coming for your daughter," the boy said in a voice that came out as two separate voices. The innocent voice of a child and the sinister voice of a death metal singer.

This made Lincoln stop and turn. He was scared shitless, but he would fight anyone, or in this case anything, that threatened his little girl. He walked back to the steps and looked down at the closed door. His hands went to his head, pulling his hair in frustration. Had that been real? He didn't know. What he did know is he wanted to get out of there, so he ran to the bottom of the steps, locked the door after struggling to close it for longer than he cared for, and ran back up. He cleaned up around his truck and drove for home. Not once did he look back.

V

June 8th, 10:40 P.M:

Edwin had spent the whole day Monday pacing back and forth in his living room. There was no way he could sleep, not after what he'd seen in the holding cell at the police station. He no longer knew exactly what he believed, but he was positive that whatever happened was unnatural. He resisted using the word supernatural, but he certainly thought it a possibility, as well.

He had received phone calls all day. Mostly comforting calls from family, friends, and coworkers, but there was also a number of death threats, too. He was told several times that if the caller found out he murdered his own son than his house would "accidently catch fire". Edwin shrugged it off. Fuck them, anyway. Who were they to have any idea what was happening in his life or his home.

The one call he had hoped to get more than any other was from his ex-wife. He didn't care so much to talk to her. Really, he would like it if he never had to talk to her again, but he hoped that she cared enough about Timothy to at least call. He wanted so badly to believe that she would know he hadn't done anything to hurt their son. He had anger issues, sure, but she would believe him. Even in bouts of rage he would never kill his son. But she never called.

As Monday transitioned unstoppably from morning to midday, afternoon into late evening, Edwin continued to pace. Only now he paced through his backyard in the dark. He wouldn't blame anyone for thinking him mad, but once again, fuck them. They probably couldn't see him anyway in the poorly lit yard. Edwin and his son had only been living in that house for six months or so, but there were plenty of good memories for him to sift through. He thought of the times he had chased Timothy through the grass. The little boy running, throwing his little arms in the air and laughing wildly, as the Tickle Monster came for his toes.

A small thud derailed his train of thought. At first he assumed it was one of the neighbors egging his house, but when he heard it again he realized it was a knock on the door. A strange hour for visitors, but he wasn't going to give these bastards the satisfaction of thinking they'd scared him. He climbed the three steps to the back porch, walked through the house, and opened the door on the other side.

"Hi, Edwin." Karen stood on the front stoop. Her blonde hair hung down past her shoulders, those blue eyes looked at him through a curtain of tears that were too stubborn to let go and roll down her cheeks.

Edwin had been hoping she would call, but he surely didn't expect her to come by, especially at this hour. "What are you doing here?" he finally asked. He wanted to be stern with her, but he didn't want to frighten her away. Having someone on his side to talk to is what he really wanted right now.

"I—I don't really know," she responded.

Edwin could tell she'd spent the day crying. Any other day she wouldn't be caught dead outside the house without makeup on and her hair done. Here she stood, her face pale and hair messy. He was only sure she'd known because his mother told him yesterday that they had spoken.

There was another pause before she finally broke the silence and said, "I'm really sorry." And with that, the floodgates opened and she embraced him.

Edwin, despite his hatred for this woman, still loved her, and holding her like this again brought back some great memories of their early relationship. An amazing combination of strawberry and kiwi filled his nostrils as he inhaled the scent of her shampoo, and her cheeks were warm and soft—also a little wet—against his own. He invited her in and sat beside her on the couch. Their hug continued for several more minutes as they worked through the tears. Finally Edwin pulled away and looked at the woman who'd once been his wife.

"You know I would never hurt him like that. Please tell me you do," Edwin begged.

"I know, Edwin. You get angry, but I know you would never get that angry. When I heard what happened . . . well, I really didn't want to believe it. The news said you are suspected of foul play, but I know you wouldn't. I know you wouldn't, Edwin. I just can't believe someone came by and snatched him away from us."

Edwin lingered on her use of the word us. Us hasn't been a thing in a long time, and she hasn't been a big part of Timothy's life in a long time. A brief flash of the day he'd left her flickered in his brain. There was a chime on his phone that told him a large purchase had just come through the bank. He opened the app and found that over six grand had just been spent on airline tickets.

In a state of confusion, he called Karen and started off by asking how things were. She had told him calmly that her and her girlfriends were having a good time. He then asked about the purchase. Was it her or identity theft?

"That was me," she replied matter-of-factly.

"Why the fuck did you spend six grand on airline tickets?" He could feel his face turning red.

"I'm taking my friends to Paris next week." Blissfully unaware. "Neither Janet nor I have been, and Beth said it's absolutely lovely. Especially this time o"

"Next fucking week?" Edwin yelled.

Before she could respond he hung up. For a while he paced the living room. He could hear Timothy in the hallway trying to figure out what was going on but wanted to leave him out of this. Storming past the little boy, Edwin went into his room and closed the door. He thought about packing, but mostly he thought about suicide. It would be so peaceful to die right now. An overdose was cleanest. Plus he could lie on Karen's side of the bed and really fuck up her night. He didn't own a gun, so that wasn't an option. Slit wrists? Hanging? Never did he realize how hard he'd been crying.

Finally, he settled on packing.

"And after the reality of him being taken away sunk in, I decided to come see you in person. I think it's better that we talk like this, face to face." Karen caressed his face with her right hand and brushed away a tear from his eye with her thumb and brought it to her lips.

Edwin thought this a bit odd, but chose to ignore it. “I’m really glad you came. I know I fucked things up pretty bad with us, and I don’t blame you for leaving.” He knew it wasn’t only him, but he had no desire to start a fight right now. “I just wish you would have been there more for Timothy.”

Karen blinked a tear from her eye and nodded as she tried to hold in another round of sobs. Taking a deep breath, she finally said, “I know. I know. He deserved a mother much better than I was. I shouldn’t have left him like that. I ignored his calls. I did everything I could to not see him because it was like looking into the face of the truth; the truth that I’m a horrible person and a much worse mother. I threw away so many chances to be the mother he deserved.”

“No, it wasn’t your fault.” He stopped as she wiped another tear from just below his right eye and brought it to her lips once again. “I know things are hard right now,” he managed to say before she did this another time, only this time with a tear that had worked its way from his left eye. “I’m sorry, why do you keep wiping my tears on your lip?” he finally had to ask, rude or not, it was getting weird.

“I miss the way you taste, Edwin.” She leaned in and kissed him deeply. Her tongue rolling across his and her hands moved right to his pants.

It had been so long since Edwin had had sex, Karen being the last, and masturbation was getting pretty old. There was a tingle in his stomach that spread to the back of his balls. Seconds later, he felt Karen’s hand wrap around him and she pulled him free of his pants. He let his head drop back against the couch as pleasure consumed him.

“I’ve really missed the way you taste,” she repeated, only this time her voice was a deep, menacing growl.

Edwin sat straight up and looked into those smoky gray sockets set in a skull so black it pulled the light from the room. The tiny red embers burning in the center of those empty eye sockets had become far more prominent in those terrible eyes now than they were when Edwin first saw them. Although the skull was the center piece of the attraction, a thin veil of smoke swirled around to form the faintest ridges of lips. He tried to scream, but she gripped his throat with her free hand—he quickly went soft in her other—and blocked his airway.

"Your tears . . . so salty . . . so sweet. But your boy's tasted much better. Much better. All of that innocence in his soul." The creature's deep, booming voice rattled his eyes and ear drums. The barely visible lips moved over the teeth as the creature talked as if their scarce existence could help form the words. Then it freed him from its grasp and stepped away.

He pulled his pants up as he gasped for air. Finally, Edwin managed to croak, "Give me my boy back."

"I told you, I can't. He's already gone." The black figure began to look much more masculine in shape as its size increased right before Edwin's eyes.

"Then what the hell do you want with me? You want to finish the job? Kill me. KILL ME! You fuck, kill me now!" Edwin screamed and sobbed. Tears rolled quickly down his face and dropped into his lap.

"I don't want you to die, Daddy," Timothy's voice said.

"You don't do that! You don't mock him!" Edwin stood up and lunged toward the monster that brought him so much pain and grief. In the brief moment before they collided he saw shock on the perpetually smoking skull. He wasn't sure if he had actually seen it or sensed it, but he knew damn well it was there.

The entities collided like two runaway trains on the same track. The pissed off father with nothing else to lose and the evil being would fight to the death. It ended now. Nothing could stop this father's rage. Edwin fell on top of the figure as it dropped to the floor. His fist collided with the black, cloudy skull, only by the time his fist struck, it was moving in slow motion. Edwin felt as if he were trying to move under water.

Staring into the black void, he saw the shock disappear, replaced with joy. But it wasn't quite joy, rather, it was some kind of mock representation done by a creature who had only ever felt pain and sorrow if it had ever truly felt anything at all. If Edwin wasn't deep in his attempts to murder this thing he may have felt sorry for it.

Besides, there wasn't any time to feel sorry for it. The black figure moved from its back to a full standing position in one unearthly motion, carrying Edwin with it. Long bony fingers wrapped tightly around Edwin's neck again, but it didn't apply any pressure. The smoky orbs examined Edwin's face as if reading a Lost Puppy flier on a telephone pole.

Curiosity?

The figure's other hand flew up against his face with unreal speed. Edwin flinched in preparation of a painful slap, but the hand slowed and gently wiped away the tears from Edwin's warm cheek. The dry, rough hand glistened with salty wetness before rubbing it into that cold, black face.

Edwin had been working up a thick wad of saliva. He inhaled quickly and blew the balled up fluid from his mouth. There was a pain in his back as he collapsed to the ground in time to see the thick puddle hit the carpet.

The beast had vanished, and Edwin lay on the carpet looking at the small wet spot of spit. Then his laughter rushed out in loud barks. He touched the damn thing. And to him that meant he could kill it.

June 9th, 12:07 P.M:

Lincoln didn't return to the church on Tuesday. He had called Pastor Simmons and told him that he had some personal business to attend to and that he would be in on Wednesday working harder than ever. The understanding pastor told him not to worry and to return back when he felt up to it and to not overwork himself when he did.

So Lincoln stayed in bed all morning, never even changing out of his pajama pants despite Kaydence telling him repeated that he looked like a bum, and even folks who weren't feeling well would feel better when they got out of their damn PJs. Around noon, when the fear of pissing the bed was on the verge of becoming a reality, he crawled out from under the covers and walked to the bathroom.

The house had been a comfortable temperature since the strange cold spell Monday morning, allowing him to walk around barefoot with no shirt on. Something Kaydence certainly enjoyed, as the hard work he did kept him in great shape despite his appetite for junk food. He knew it would catch up with him sooner or later, but as long as he could eat whatever the hell he wanted and still look this good, he was going to eat.

He pissed for a solid three minutes, a world record he was sure, but he would be disappointed to find out it was far from it. While washing his hands, he looked into the mirror, but it wasn't himself that looked back, the dark figure—nothing more than a shadow version of himself—stared back at him. The figure wasn't behind or in front of him. It had replaced him.

Lincoln stumbled backward, tripping over the stool Sadie stood on to brush her teeth. The back of his head hit the wall, making his vision flutter briefly. It wasn't enough to keep him down; however, as he stood up and faced the creature in the mirror. It moved when he moved. It leaned when he leaned. He started to feel like he was in an old Warner Bros. cartoon.

"You stay the fuck away from my family. Do you hear me?" Lincoln said and watched in curiosity as the figure appeared to say the words with him. Only its eyes stood out on its otherwise featureless, yet skull-like face. They were like the campfire smoke you just can't escape not matter what side of the fire you move to. He couldn't escape them. The smoke rolled perpetually in an invisible ball. He felt as if this creature toyed with him, and he didn't like it. "Fuck you," he said before punching the mirror. Broken shards of mirror, pill bottles, and a toothpaste tube fell into the sink and scattered across the marble countertop.

He leaned over the sink, planted his palms to the wall, and glared down at the mess. The blood from his knuckles trickled briskly down his arm before dripping from his elbow, splattering like red raindrops in the broken chaos below. Luckily Kaydence and Sadie Elizabeth had gone to the store. He wouldn't hear the end of this one for a month if they'd been home.

Grabbing the bathroom trashcan, he threw away the glass and put everything away in the medicine cabinet. He cleaned up the blood and bandaged his knuckles while thinking of a way to explain what had happened. Maybe this afternoon he'd run into town and buy a new cabinet to play it off as a plan. This one had come from a renovation he'd done a year or so ago. The homeowners said they'd rather he keep what he wanted instead of seeing it in the trash. He definitely loved doing renovations for people like that.

He walked downstairs and sat at the small table in the breakfast nook. It was lunch time, but he wasn't all that hungry. Lincoln grabbed the Muscatine Journal instead and prepared to thumb through it. He wasn't big on the news, but there was usually something interesting. The article on the front page, reserved for the best stories, of course, caught his eye.

The house was one that sat across from the church where he had been working, and the story headline: Local Boy Still Missing After Mysterious Disappearance, sent a chill down his spine. He read the article, put the paper down, then picked it up and read the article again. Lincoln stared at the paper, focusing on the description of the boy. It matched that of the boy in the church basement. For a moment, he thought about calling the police, but then he remembered the unusual circumstances surrounding his run in with the boy. What he thought he saw could get a man thrown in the Mireside Mental Institution. Instead, he settled on calling the pastor and having him check on things in the basement. Perhaps the boy had run away from home and was playing a joke on Lincoln. Hopefully the pastor would run into the boy and send him home.

Reaching for his phone, Lincoln continued to look at the house in the picture, a white two-story with police caution tape across the door. But there was more; a figure could be seen in the second floor window, a little boy standing in a dark room? Probably just a reflection from when the photo was taken; however, Lincoln couldn't take his eyes off it. He felt drawn in, like wherever he moved his eyes, they would focus themselves on the figure.

Tossing the paper down again, Lincoln walked over to the Stuff Drawer, the bottom drawer in the island at the center of the kitchen. He shuffled through the scissors, screwdrivers, tape, and other junk until he found what he was looking for. A magnifying glass, a purchase for Sadie when she wanted a closer look at the lightning bugs they caught last summer.

Lincoln sat down and grabbed the paper. He looked through the magnifying glass, and was shocked to see that the figure was gone. He checked the other windows although he was sure it was that one. Dropping the paper, he rubbed his eyes. Maybe he was losing it. Taking in a deep breath through his nose, he smelt that oily smell from earlier. His eyes shot opened and he looked around the kitchen. The place was empty except for him, but when he looked back down at the paper, the figure was back, only now it was standing in the window next to the front door of the house.

He brought the magnifying glass back up, expecting the figure to be gone, but now it stood in the doorway, the door now open where it wasn't a moment ago. "Oh shit," he said. His heart started to race as he examined the small figure. It was so quiet he could hear his heart beating in his chest like a machine gun. He couldn't take his eyes off what he was sure was the missing boy. And he was sure that boy was the one in the basement.

The black figure of the little boy stood in the doorway for only a moment longer. Then it ran toward Lincoln. His movement was choppy, like a flip book being thumbed through slowly, and before Lincoln could react, the child reached up through the newspaper photo and started pulling himself out. His flesh was lifeless and pale and looked as if it would be cold to the touch. Set deep in the boy's skull were eyes that were orbs of smoke rolling like storm clouds. That oncoming storm seemed to bore deep into Lincoln's soul. Blood from the boy's matted hair dripped onto the table, blotting out the black print of the newspaper.

An intense heat radiated from the boy despite how cold

he appeared, and he spoke in a deep, watery voice. "Her soul will be ours, Lincoln. And you can take a place at my side. At my side is where you belong."

His small fingers squeezed the man's throat, and Lincoln was bombarded with visions: a magnificent creature surrounded by a beauty even the most talented and imaginative renaissance artists would fail to capture. The features below its smooth head are neither male nor female, but there is more magnificence in that face than any mortal could understand in a lifetime of trying. Long wings of the most majestic feathers reflected a brilliant light from an unseen, perhaps omnipresent source as they stretched to the being's feet.

Than the light—more white and pure than any on Earth—falls away as if it's forbidden from touching this stunning beast, leaving a darkness so black it inflicts physical pain on the glorious being.

In the darkness, the once beautiful creature is distorted and twisted into something sinister. Something wretched. The exquisitely delicate flesh cracks and flakes away, leaving a rough grayish brown hide. Blood streaks down the now hideous face as long black horns erupt from its skull. The wings catch fire, burning fast and bright, leaving behind charred feathers. Still in pain, it rises up; the once smooth feet now heavy black hooves that clack loudly against the scorching rock. Behind this repugnant horror, a blackened army marches fiercely to greet their long awaited general.

Pain erupts in Lincoln's head. His eyes bleed and his skin burns as if he'd been doused with acid. All of his fingers curled backward at the knuckles until his fingernails dug into the top of his hands. Blood soaked through his socks as the phalanges and metatarsals in his feet exploded, sending shards of broken bones tearing through the skin like shrapnel. As he felt his scalp liquefy and run down his neck he released a horrified scream that at first sounded muffled but quickly built up power as he found the oxygen his lunges craved.

"Lincoln!" Kaydence screamed as she ran into the kitchen. "Oh God, are you alright?"

Lincoln looked up into her terrified face. Her mouth hung open. One hand was on her chest while the other gripped Lincoln's shoulder. He could see Sadie standing at the kitchen entryway where her mom had dropped several bags of groceries, along with the jug of milk that poured its contents to the floor.

"Are you ok, Daddy?" she asked but stayed where she was.

"Yeah," he replied in a dry voice. "Daddy's fine." The words hung up in his throat briefly before finding their way out into the surrounding air. He swallowed hard, smiled, and looked into Kaydence's eyes. "I'm fine. Must've dozed off."

"Lincoln, if something's going on, you need to tell me. You've been acting very strange since your nightmare the other night."

"I'm fine. Really! I was just reading this article about the missing boy, must've day dreamed about losing Sadie." Lincoln held up the paper for Kaydence to see the article.

She grabbed the paper from him. "Which article?" She turned a few pages as she asked.

"The front page article, a boy is missing from just across the street from the church I'm working at. Something like that happening right next to where I'm working just hit really close to home." He pointed a finger to the front page and said, "Right here."

"Junior High Fundraiser A Huge Success?" she asked with a little confusion.

Lincoln ripped the paper away from her, his temper flaring. "Right fucking here!" he screamed. He froze in dumb wonder. He looked at the front page photo of a group of students selling baked goods to raise money for the new library addition.

Kaydence tried not to look hurt. "I didn't fucking deserve that!"

Lincoln stood up and tried to wrap his arms around his wife in comfort, but she pushed away. "I'm sorry. It must be in another paper. I'm really sorry." He walked over and tried to help her pick the groceries up off the floor. Sadie had run upstairs to avoid seeing her parents fight, leaving the bags she carried lying on the floor.

"Get away from me, Lincoln. I don't want your help." She smacked a bag from his hand. The carton of eggs hit the floor, half of the white ovals rolled out; half of those cracked, oozing out into the milk puddle.

Throwing his arms up, Lincoln said, "Fine," and walked upstairs to check on Sadie. Fights between Edwin and Kaydence were rare, but when they did happen Sadie Elizabeth could shut down for hours.

His daughter's bedroom door was open, and he saw her lying in bed when he walked in. The doll was held firmly in her arms, and upon seeing it the hair on his arms stood up. He felt as if it watched him. The closer he stepped to his daughter the colder the air around him became. By the time he stood directly in front of her, he was shivering.

"Sadie, are you ok?" He reached down to touch her, but just before he did her eyes shot open, revealing only smooth white, like tiny cue balls that haven't yet seen their first billiards game.

"I am watching over her soul now," she said in her own voice. "You will not take it."

Lincoln didn't know how to respond, a part of him felt as if she wasn't even talking to him. His daughter looked up into his eyes, and he felt an evil presence all around him. "I will fight for my daughter. You let her go, now." The words came out more frail than he had intended. He was scared, and he had certainly been in his share of fights, winning most, but he wasn't even sure how to fight whatever was happening here.

"I command you to leave this place, for your own good," Sadie said, her voice still her own but something on the very edge of her words was not. "You're not strong enough to fight the dem—"

"You can't have her!" he screamed and began shaking her violently. "You stay away from her!"

A brief flicker of the fear on the little girl's face was all Lincoln caught before a force far stronger than himself flung his body to the floor. Blackness crept across the walls of Sadie's room, as if an artist spilled his paint on the canvas and rotated it to watch it run and give it the freedom to be whatever it chose. Then pain exploded in his abdomen, and he saw Kaydence standing above him. She drove her bare foot, heel first, into his stomach. Sadie sat on her bed and bawled.

"You don't ever touch her! I'll kill you! You touch her like that again and I'll fucking kill you, Lincoln." Kaydence was crying harder than Sadie was as she pummeled the man on the floor. "You get the fuck out before I call the cops. NOW!" She kicked him back to the ground as he tried to climb to his feet. "Forget that, I'm not going to call anyone. I'm just going to kick the shit out of you, you fucking prick!"

"What the fuck!" Lincoln yelled as he gasped for breath. "Stop it, settle the fuck down. It's not what you think." He held his hand out in defense as his wife, much smaller than him, continued her relentless assault. "Listen to me!"

"I don't want to hear it! You have five minutes, Lincoln. Grab whatever you need and leave." She pushed him out of the bedroom and slammed the door so hard it sounded like a gunshot went off and the wood splintered up the middle.

Lincoln had to struggle to get to his feet, but finally managed. For a few moments he stood staring at the cracked door leading into his daughter's room. Reaching out, he tried to knock but thought better of it. He walked to his bedroom, loaded a duffle bag with some clothes, and headed out for his truck. He tossed the bag over to the passenger's side of the bench seat and climbed in. The truck started with a turn of the ignition, and he stared at the house for a minute before slamming the shifter into reverse. As he backed down the driveway, he looked up at the window in Sadie's room. His little girl stood in the window watching him, her hand pressed to the glass.

Behind her in the shadows stood a figure Lincoln couldn't quite see. At first he believed it to be Kaydence, but her hair was shorter than this shadow figure. He briefly dismissed it as a strange effect of the lighting, and it was nothing more than Kaydence's shadow, but then Kaydence stepped through the figure into view and it dissipated in a thin mist.

He stopped the truck and jumped out to run back to the house when he heard a single hollow knock from above him. He looked up to see Sadie glance up at her mother. Kaydence had smacked the window and shook her head angrily at Lincoln as their eyes met. Lincoln held his arms out to gesture how ridiculous this whole thing was, but Kaydence flipped him off, and pulled their daughter away from the window.

Climbing back into the truck made his heart sink as he realized he would be driving down the long driveway after the first, and certainly strangest, fight he and Kaydence had had in a very long time. He wasn't sure where he would go, but he had plenty of daylight left to burn. Most of his friends and family lived in the area, but the last thing he wanted was to burden them with a night's stay. Really he was just too embarrassed to tell anyone he'd been kicked out of his house, so he decided on heading back to the church to work the afternoon away. After that he'd be sleeping in his truck on the street outside the church, parked where Pastor Simmons wouldn't see him.

He pulled off Highway 38 and into a gas station parking lot, stopping next to one of the gas pumps.

A teenage girl stood beside a white Dodge Avenger at the pump across from him. She was staring down at her phone while waiting on her car to fill but looked up at Lincoln and gave him a smile and a nod before brushing her wavy brown hair from her face and returning to her phone. He returned the silent greeting and ran his debit card through the card reader of the pump.

"You're going to burn in Hell, you know." The voice was young, sweet, and oddly cold.

Lincoln froze for a second, looked around for the source of the voice and hoped it wasn't the nice young girl on the other side of the pumps. He shook it off. Perhaps she'd been talking to her phone in response to a text from an ex-boyfriend.

"I'm coming for your wife and daughter. Such sweet girls you have in your life. I'm going to peel the flesh from their bodies and feast on their guts." Exquisite composure.

This time Lincoln knew this was directed toward him.

He leaned around the pump to confront the teenager, but she was no longer standing by her car. The gas nozzle was lying on the ground spilling its flammable liquid in a wide puddle across the concrete.

"Shit," Lincoln barked. Jumping across, he picked the nozzle up off the ground and released the locking clip to stop the gas flow. He flipped the lever down and placed the nozzle back on the pump. Looking around, the teenage girl was still nowhere to be found.

Trying to glance through the store's large front windows to see if she'd gone inside and left the pump unattended, he realized he had done the same thing. Walking back round the pump just in time for his nozzle to shut off on its own with a click, Lincoln flipped his lever down and replaced the nozzle on his side.

He walked into the store to inform the clerk that there had been some fuel spilled by a careless teen, but he was shocked to see that the teen from outside was standing behind the counter soaking wet. His brain sent up the red flag before he even smelled the strong odor of gasoline.

"Miss, you need to come outside with me," Lincoln urged. He held out his hands for her despite being on opposite sides of the counter. "Do you work here?"

No response. The teenager watched him vigilantly as he moved further into the store.

"Where is the clerk? Is there someone else working here?" The words came out harsh as the gas fumes worked into his lungs. "Please come outside with me. There's a water hose outside. We can get the gas rinsed off and call an ambulance."

As he continued to move closer he realized she hadn't blinked since he walked in. Her eyes were completely red and thin lines of blood trickled down from the inside of her upper eyelids.

Coming around the corner to the opening in the counter, Lincoln saw an older woman lying on the floor. Her neck was completely smashed after repeatedly being stomped on. Small fragments of bone poked through the skin and both of her eyes bulged out in terror. The teenager had caught her by surprise despite reeking of gasoline. The teenager's left foot was covered in blood, as well as gas.

"Oh shit," Lincoln gasped. He looked from the dead woman to the girl. "You need to stop this."

"Give me her soul, and I will. Nobody else has to die," the girl said. She continued to speak unemotionally, as if she were desensitized to the situation. It had been several minutes, and she still hadn't blinked.

Lincoln was becoming light-headed from the fumes.

The girl reached across the counter and grabbed a lighter from an orange display case. A sick smile spread across her face.

"Please don't. Come outside with me now," he begged.

Bringing the lighter up to her chin, the girl's thumb spun the striker wheel across the flint. The moment the orange flame lit up under her chin her entire face erupted in flames. Small bursts of flames popped in the air around them, igniting the pockets of fumes, but the majority of the fire remained on the girl as her entire body was quickly engulfed.

The screams that escaped her were enough for Lincoln to know that whatever monster had caused her to do this had left in time for her to suffer. Darting past the girl, Lincoln grabbed a small fire extinguisher from behind the counter and coated her in the powdery spray.

With the fire out, he dropped the red canister and gawked helplessly down at the girl's burnt corpse. Her skin still bubbled in places. In others, blood pooled and ran to the floor. What was once her long, wavy brown hair was now short black threads. The smell of her burning flesh and hair, mixed with the already nauseating feeling of the gas fumes was enough to make Lincoln charge outside and vomit. When he was finished he called the police.

It took several hours of sitting in the back of a police car before Lincoln was cleared to go. They'd reviewed the security footage and confirmed Lincoln's story, but he would still be contacted within the next few days for further questioning.

He told them that reliving the ordeal was something he didn't want to do, but he'd be available anytime they needed him to be.

With most of the afternoon now behind him, he drove until sundown and parked in front of the church. Using the duffle bag as a pillow, he tossed and turned on the seat of his truck, knowing that he would not be sleeping tonight. If he ever slept again it'd be a miracle.

Several hours inched by painfully before Lincoln's body finally won over his mind, and he drifted off into a light sleep. But just as that light sleep finally touched him, he was abruptly woken by a thud on the roof of the truck. He sat up lazily and peered out the windows, examining his surroundings with the curiosity of a child. The night was calm, but he could tell by the trees across the street that the wind blew gently from the south and probably brushed something out of a tree above. He laid his head back down and closed his eyes.

Thud.

This one happened seconds after his eyes closed, and he felt it rock the truck. He sat up and prepared to push the driver's door open when a hand, mutilated and bloody, smacked into the windshield, making a sickening splat sound. At first, he thought it belonged to whoever was on the roof of his pickup, but then he realized the hand was at the bottom of the glass with the fingers pointing upward.

A second hand hit the passenger's side window, followed by a third to the rear glass. The splattery-smacks came consistently as more hands appeared on the windows around the truck. Each one angled differently. Each one was bloody. The blood, to Lincoln's amazement, ran *up* the glass, laughing in the face of gravity.

"What do you want?" he yelled. "You can't have my daughter!"

As in response, the hands—remaining angled as they were—slid up the windows. There was squeaking from the decayed, bloody flesh as it rubbed across the smooth glass. Lincoln pushed the door open and hopped to the ground, took several steps, and turned to face the truck. The boy stood on the roof amidst his gut pile that squirmed as if it was a living being of its own. Lincoln pictured the snake breeding balls he'd seen on National Geographic.

"You stay away from her," Lincoln ordered.

"Let Him save her soul," the little boy said. The look on his dead face was hurried, as if he didn't have much time, and his light-blue eyes were so brilliant they almost radiated light.

"Timothy? Timmy, right? I read about you in the paper. Or are you something else, pretending to be that little boy? I'm not letting anyone harm her. Do you hear me?"

The boy tried to speak but started choking and a lump worked its way up his throat. His jaw dropped down, cracking and grinding as it overextended, and a thin black hand emerged from his mouth. In the grotesque hand was the hunk of meat that was the boy's tongue. It dangled lifelessly before being dropped into the gut pile.

Instead of the shock Lincoln expected to see in the boy's eyes, there was a sick pleasure. Those brilliant blue eyes were sucked back into the little face only to be replaced by smooth spheres of black storm clouds. It made Lincoln think of one friend taking off a mask and handing it to another to try on if the other friend was a fucking demon.

"I wish someone would have told me never to play with fire." The boy's mouth moved, but the words coming out were that of the teenage girl at the gas station. "Don't let me burn, Lincoln." This was playfully spoken and sickening for Lincoln to hear. "That would be a terrible way for a young girl to die."

A deep laugh escaped the boy's throat but didn't echo. It felt heavy in the air and at the same time hollow.

"Lincoln?"

His name being called from behind him caused him to jump and spin around preparing to counter whatever attack may be coming.

Pastor Simmons walked into the parking lot. "Is everything alright?" He had a look on his face that was a little too knowing for Lincoln to ignore. Fear laced with a hint of something that Lincoln felt was anticipation.

VI

June 10th, 5:00 A.M:

"Did you see him? I think it's the boy from next door. I've seen him in the basement, as well." Lincoln begged the question more than asked as Pastor Simmons approached him from the direction of the church. What at first appeared to be an incredibly dark night was now somehow filled with pre-dawn light. "Tell me you saw him just now."

"Lincoln," Pastor Simmons started, sounding hesitant.

"You can't think I'm making this up!" Lincoln was growing tired of this. He was either nuts or he wasn't, and he wanted to know which it was now.

"I saw the boy, Lincoln." Pastor Simmons looked at Lincoln with tired eyes. They weren't the tired eyes of a sleepy man, but those of a man who'd seen far too much in his life, a man who had fought hard battles, and came out victorious only to admit defeat because of the things he'd lost in those battles. Lincoln was sure the pastor had a quote in him along the lines of a war won where lives are lost is no victory at all.

Lincoln couldn't speak. His mouth hung open stupidly, as if he'd just been told the great secret of life. Relief washed over him, yet at the same time he'd rather be crazy. He knew he could protect his family from crazy. There was no telling if he could protect his family from anything else.

"We need to talk inside, although I fear this demon's power is far too great to be hindered even in the house of God."

Lincoln wiped a bit of drool from his lip and followed the pastor into the church through a side entrance. They walked down a hallway and into an office where Pastor Simmons stood before a bookshelf built into the wall. He reached for a large hardcover book and pulled it from the shelf. The book appeared to be brand new, picked up at the midnight release just last week.

"This is an ancient text with thousands of untold stories

of Jesus Christ," he began.

Lincoln burst into a laughter that sounded almost as insane as he felt. "*That* is an ancient text?" He pointed at the cover. "That book is new. You could have gotten it anywhere. Ancient texts are usually a bit more, you know, ancient."

Pastor Simmons smiled and opened it, revealing its pearl white pages. "Don't judge a book by its cover, my friend. Every Keeper must write his own copy. I chose this cover myself." He held it up for Lincoln to see. There was a gold image of a circle with a cross inside on the cover. Gently touching the bottom of the circle was the tip of a five-pointed star that housed a black stone in the center.

"I've seen that before. There was a box in the basement, with a doll in it. It had that same symbol on it." Lincoln couldn't take his eyes off the book.

"Yes, this symbol represents the Order of Onyx and Light, sometimes simply called the Onyx Light, a group over two-thousand years old. The circle represents the eternity of God. The cross, of course, represents the sacrifice Jesus made to save humanity. Some say it is a representation of where God's love and His justice intersect. The star of Bethlehem represents Jesus' incarnation. And the onyx set into the star, well that's the story here.

"Anyway, Lincoln, I've been tasked, by the Keeper before me, to protect a sacred artifact left on this world by Jesus."

"The Holy Grail?" Lincoln blurted out.

The pastor laughed. "No. That, I'm sad to say, is somewhere else, being guarded by another powerful organization. Jesus was a great man, as you are well aware, I'm sure. He healed the sick and used his carpentry skills to help people in need. He taught the word of God, but he was also an exorcist, protecting the world from the evil entities that sought to take over the souls of the innocent."

Lincoln nodded to show he was listening. He did recall hearing of Jesus' exorcisms, but hadn't thought they were that literal.

"I'm also sure then, that you know of Judas Iscariot."

"Yeah, he was the Apostle that betrayed Jesus, leading to the crucifixion." Lincoln felt pretty confident in his answer.

"Not exactly accurate but exactly what you are expected to believe. Anyway, Jesus and Judas set out to exorcise a demon from a little girl named Adina. Jesus failed, costing the little girl her life. To Jesus and Judas, the exorcism only lasted a few minutes, but the rest of the world spun on at a more rapid pace. In reality, their battle with this creature lasted two days. Adina's life wasn't the heftiest price paid; however, her soul, along with that of the demon, was trapped in the girl's favorite doll, Bethesda.

"Shortly after their encounter, Jesus began searching for a way to free the girl's soul. Adina would be able to rest eternally in Heaven while the demon would be imprisoned forever. Day after day, week after week even, he worked to uncover a way to save that girl. There were other matters he needed to attend to, as well. Humanity was in turmoil. Hatred and sin were consuming the world, as it had done in the past. God became exhausted and displeased with this and wanted to send down His wrath once again to wipe out the world.

"Jesus, however, *believed* in humanity and the power of love. He'd seen it first hand and begged his father to forgive the people. That's when he realized that the answers he sought could not be found on Earth because they didn't exist on Earth. He knew he would have to die to save Adina, but he also knew that his death could be the beginning to saving all of mankind. It wasn't easy, but he convinced Judas to betray him, knowing that he, Jesus, would be crucified. His pain would be a sacrifice for humanity, while his death would open the passageway to finding the answers needed to save the girl.

"After the crucifixion, his body was placed in a tomb with the doll, and in his death, he sought the girl and the demon. For three days he journeyed in the dark regions of a world between life and death. What he'd learned was that Adina and the demon had fused into one being. They were now Bethesda. Jesus battled the demon Bethesda on a stygian version of Calvary Hill, the very spot his life, in our world, had ended days earlier. With the power of God, he could have defeated the demon, but the girl's soul would have been lost, thrust alongside the demon into whatever fiery pit it had crawled out of. So he backed down and was able to contain this new entity with the hopes that a way to separate the two would one day be found.

"Judas, the only Apostle to know about Bethesda, a man who had been shunned for his 'betrayal', was given orders from Jesus to guard the doll until the demon could be defeated and the girl saved. Judas started the Order of Onyx and Light, and the doll, like so many other great religious artifacts, was handed down the line." The pastor rubbed the small onyx with his thumb. "The onyx represents the sacrifice Judas made. A humble and devout follower of Christ would forever be known as a greedy wretch of a man with a heart as black as onyx. This act pushed Judas away from the friends he had grown to love as brothers." Pastor Simmons drifted off in thought for a moment.

"So why isn't this taught in church? Why do we have to have a betrayer?" asked Lincoln.

The pastor shrugged. "I teach the history they wanted us to teach."

Lincoln leaned against the doorframe, taking in what he was just told. "So you sent me to work on the basement knowing that this thing was down there?" He thought he saw a brief flicker of knowing on the pastor's face, maybe it had been guilt.

"I was unaware of the box's exact location, Lincoln. The secrets of the Onyx Light are passed down from Keeper to apprentice. My Keeper taught me all the secrets but one. Unfortunately, he passed away before he could tell me where the box had been hidden. I *am* truly sorry about all of this." Pastor Simmons looked at the floor. "I believed it to be hidden somewhere much harder to stumble upon than an old brick pillar."

Lincoln said, "So you'll be able to do something though,

right? You know how to stop this thing and protect my family?"

Pastor Simmons turned his gaze to Lincoln, who twirled his goatee in his fingers as he continued to stand by the door. "I'm terribly sorry," the pastor whispered. Lincoln could see that his mind was working. He hoped the man was looking for answers but felt instead he sought lies. "You found the box, and it opened for you. So in the eyes of the demon, you are the barrier it must tear down to escape the doll completely."

A shockwave jolted through Lincoln's body. "You can't expect me to stop it! I'm not a part of your secret party. You said *you* were the guard, not me! It's not my fault you failed, and now this . . . demon is after my daughter." Lincoln felt his fingernails digging into his palms and relaxed a little.

"I can help you, but I won't be able to fight this thing for you. Just know that until it frees itself completely from the earthly bindings of the doll, it can only do minimal damage, which is still quite a bit more than anyone would like to deal with. Once it's free, however, it will work toward ruling this world."

Lincoln thought hard about what the pastor had just said. "The boy from across the street, it was him on my truck."

"Ah, Timothy. That poor, poor boy. I hadn't suspected his disappearance to be anything but a tragic loss." The pastor pondered this briefly.

"Maybe his father knows something. He had to have seen something that will help. I'll walk over there later this morning and see what he knows," Lincoln said with a newfound hope.

"No!" Pastor Simmons snapped vigorously before backing off. "I mean, he's suffered a terrible loss. You don't want to go over there now and cause any more pain."

Lincoln looked at the pastor and watched a bead of sweat roll down out of his gray hair. He couldn't help but think the room was awfully cool to cause perspiration. The more he watched the pastor, the more nervous the older man appeared to look. "Ok," Lincoln said. "I have work to do, anyway. I'll go ahead and get started for the day. I highly doubt I'll be getting anymore sleep anytime soon."

"Sounds like a plan, my friend. I need to run to town here in a few hours and pick up a few things for tonight. Will you be alright down there by yourself, or should I wait until you take a break?" The friendly concern had returned to the older man's voice.

"I'll be fine. I'm not going to be doing anything too strenuous, just hauling out the old bricks." Without another word, Lincoln walked out of the office and headed down the hallway toward the side entrance they'd come in through. Stepping into the cool morning air, he stopped, cleared his mind, than eyeballed his truck for any signs of demons or ghosts.

Satisfied that he was alone, he climbed in his truck and drove it around to the side of the church with the basement door. As he drove around, he looked at the house that was in yesterday's newspaper one minute and gone the next.

While Lincoln worked the early morning away down in the basement, he did what he could to make sure he spent a majority of the time outside. He hauled half-loads of bricks until the pastor drove away in a decade old station wagon. Half-assing his way through a project wasn't something he'd normally do, so quite often he'd remind himself to slow back down as his pace picked up. After slowly stacking the bricks, giving the pastor time to get out of town, Lincoln walked across Maple Street.

June 10th, 9:40 A.M:

Edwin heard the knock at the front door and almost decided not to answer it. The last visitor he had was only a cruel trick played on him by this sick fuck of a monster. There was no way of knowing that this wasn't another such trick; however, Edwin sensed a bit of hesitation in the knock, as if whoever was there was having second thoughts about whether it was the best time to stop by or not. He grabbed a baseball bat, just in case, and walked to the door.

"I'm Lincoln Scott. I'm very sorry to bother you, but I

think we need to talk."

Edwin didn't recognize the man, but he almost appeared homeless. His clothes were dirty and his long goatee did nothing to persuade the much more conservative man who'd answered the door that this was a reputable human being. Certainly no monster would attempt to disguise itself as a bum.

"I have nothing to say at this time. I don't have any money for handouts. Try the church across the street." The door cried out with a hollow smack as it was slammed shut.

"Prick," Lincoln said and knocked again.

The door shot open and this time Edwin had his bat raised and ready to strike. Rage roared in his eyes. "I already told you to go the fuck away!"

Taking a shuffled step backward and raising his arms defensively, Lincoln quickly stated, "I've seen your son!"

The bat choked out a wooden knock as it bounced off the floor in the entryway. What Edwin just heard had caught him completely off guard, but then he was filled with anger. "Is this some kind of sick joke? You and the rest of your looky—loo buddies think it's funny to torment me?"

"No! No, I swear. I've seen him."

Edwin looked hard into the man's eyes. He wasn't the best judge of character, but surely he knew enough cues to look for to determine if this homeless man was lying to him or not. It took a moment before he felt the rage subside, but he also thought that if this was a prank, there would be nobody to witness the beating he'd give this man if they were in the house. "Come in and tell me what you know."

It took Lincoln a few minutes to tell Edwin about the two encounters he'd had with Timothy. During his brief yet unbelievable story, he wondered at what point this man would brain him with that baseball bat. Surprisingly, however, Edwin seemed pretty calm and understanding, taking in everything that was told to him. Most of the gory bits flooded Edwin's memory with how he'd seen his son in the holding cell. Lincoln did leave out everything about the doll, the church, and what the pastor had said, but he did say that there were some things going on with his daughter.

"So you think that this is a demon and it's using Timothy's body to communicate with you somehow. But why? Why you? It seems like a much more *demony* thing to do to torment *me* that way."

"Look, I know it sounds nuts, but it's the truth, and I really don't know why this is happening to me." He wanted to bring up everything the pastor had told him, but he thought it best to move forward with this in baby steps and get a feel for this man before frying his senses with a horror movie overload.

"This is going to sound *more* nuts, but I believe you." Edwin looked at Lincoln the way a father might look at his son while telling his son how much he loves him despite grounding him for being out all night.

Another knock on the door caused both men to start. Edwin grabbed his bat and walked right up to the front door. In one motion, he turned the knob and pulled the door open.

"Hello, Mr. Carmichael," Officer Martinez said solemnly. Officer Stevens stood behind him. "How are you doing?"

"I'm about as fine as I can be," Edwin answered. He looked first at Officer Martinez, than to Stevens. They seemed to be the real deal, but who knew.

"We just wanted to come by and check on you. We haven't heard from you in a few days," Stevens said. The tone in his voice was almost incriminating. Edwin got the feeling that after having time to clear his head, Stevens started to doubt what he'd seen in the holding cell. Probably by convincing himself it'd been a long night.

"But we wanted to apologize, we haven't gotten in touch with you, either," Martinez jumped in. "We've been really busy with this case. Both of us, along with a number of other officers, have been pulling double shifts. We're going to find your boy."

Stevens caught a glimpse of Lincoln walking through the living room. "Who's that?" he asked and pushed his way through the door.

"Oh, sorry," Lincoln said. He spoke quickly as the officer moved toward him. "I'm Lincoln Scott. I've been working across the street at the church, doing renovations in the basement. Mr. Carmichael saw me working and was kind enough to invite me over for a drink." He quickly added, "Water, of course."

"Of course," Officer Stevens said and backed out of the house, both his hands in the air. The untrusting eyes taking in everything they could in the short amount of time they had. "We'll be in touch, and remember to call us if you *think* of anything else you'd like to tell us." The look on the officer's face told Edwin that the gears were spinning inside that brain of his, and Edwin had the feeling they were turning the wrong way.

"I'd like to check that church basement when we have the chance," Stevens said when they climbed into the police cruiser.

"Why?" Martinez asked from the driver's seat.

"I have a theory: Mr. Carmichael wants to be rid of his son, notices this man working at the church, and hires him to kill his son and bury him in the walls or floor of the basement. Your buddy Edwin makes damn good money. A lot more than a guy doing side jobs for extra cash."

Martinez had worked with Stevens for several years now. They had always gotten along fine, but he was really starting to feel that this case was going to break his partner. "I don't know if I agree. You know I mean no offense. I've always admired and looked up to you as my partner, but I think that guy's reno business is pretty popular. I bet he makes tons of money. He wouldn't need Edwin's money."

Stevens shot him a quick how-dare-you glance and thought better of snapping on him. "How about this: We'll stop by the church tonight; the doors will be open for their Wednesday prayers and whatnot. Then we just head on down into the basement and take a peek around. If there isn't anything down there then I'll drop it."

"Fine with me, "Martinez said and backed out onto the street and drove off.

As Edwin watched the cruiser drive down the street, he

saw the black figure, Karen, and Timothy sitting in the back. The three turned to him and waved as if they were off on a family vacation and Edwin was staying behind to house-sit. Edwin watched them until they turned out of sight before turning to face Lincoln, who stood right behind him. The blood had drained from both their faces.

"I saw it, too," Lincoln said.

"I'm tired of that fucker using my boy for its twisted games. I'm going to stop it, and it best hope demons can't feel pain," Edwin said through clenched teeth.

June 10th, 7:25 P.M:

"Alright, we can make this quick," Martinez said. "We should be able to tell what work is new and what isn't pretty easily. So we can at least narrow our search that way."

Officer Alex Martinez had always held himself to the highest standards of Protect and Serve. His faith in the law was unwavering despite the fact that he knew the justice system was in shambles. It would all work itself out, and until it did, he would be needed by the honest people of this county.

He hadn't believed that either man had anything to do with Timothy's disappearance, and after what Stevens had told him he saw in the holding cell, he couldn't believe his partner truly thought they had. Martinez hadn't told his partner, but he and Edwin had met the day before and talked. Nothing more than "shootin' the shit" as his father would have put it, but it felt good, and that talk gave him a pretty solid idea about what kind of man Edwin was. For now, however, he would humor Stevens, knowing they wouldn't find anything, but if they did . . .

"We won't need much time anyway. I'll find where those bastards hid the body," Stevens stated.

The two officers walked relatively unhindered into the church, being waved at by only two little girls, and down the stairs to the basement. At the bottom of the stairs, they lifted the thick plastic draped from the top of the entryway. They were instantly hit with the smell of decay and the copper smell of blood. Stevens pointed to his nose and gave Martinez an I-told-you-so nod. Martinez wasn't completely convinced, but his brain prepared him for the inevitable betrayal he'd feel, not only toward Edwin, but from his own damn intuition.

Lincoln had gone home two hours earlier with the hopes of apologizing to Kaydence. He had completed the work on the pillar in the center. It would, however, remain supported by the jacks until the mortar set. The officers sat in the cruiser down the street and watched the man load up his tools in the back of his Chevy pickup before heading off.

Now the basement was quiet, and Martinez had been right about telling the difference. The new brickwork stuck out like the difference between night and day. The smell worsened as the two men crept further into the large room. New bricks were stacked neatly in one corner, while old bricks were cluttered around a hand cart that stood by the stairs.

Martinez, who had just moved to an upstairs apartment, admired the cart. There were three smaller wheels on a triangular bracket instead of one wheel on each side that allowed the cart to climb up and down the stairs with ease. If only he'd had one a month ago. His back has been slightly sore since.

"Check this out," Stevens said as he stopped in the center of the room where the fresh pillar sat with a large floor jack on each side. "I bet this is where the boy's body is. Perfect place for it if you ask me."

"Be careful with that. It may be there for support." The worry in Martinez' voice was thick.

"All the better for hiding a body."

Martinez felt this was becoming more of a blind vendetta than any real investigation. But there *was* the smell of blood to consider, and this made him wonder if maybe Stevens was right.

"Help me with this," Stevens said as he grabbed a pipe and drove it into the brick pillar. With each loud clang of steel on concrete, he stopped and listened, breath held.

They could hear murmurs from the floor above them. Some children were singing; others played games based on bible stories. Parents chatted with each other in the hallways. Trying to stir up envy from their friends with their new car or their child's A+ report card. It seemed as if none of them paid any attention to the sounds from the basement, if they'd even heard it. Perhaps they'd known there was work being done, and assumed it was the contractors.

The first brick broke free as the mortar, although quick setting still hadn't completely dried. It fell inward and landed with a cushioned thud that made Stevens jerk his gaze to Martinez, his eyes widened in an almost crazed delight as if he were an archeologist that finally found the tomb he'd searched his entire life for. The hieroglyphics were purposely misleading, but Stevens managed to decipher them correctly.

Stevens leaned closer but quickly withdrew and stepped away to vomit. It splashed on the floor, causing Martinez to hop back as chunks of Stevens' diner splattered toward his shiny black boots.

"Are you alright?" Martinez asked, keeping his distance.

"Yeah, that smell . . . it's fucking awful."

Martinez did notice that the smell grew much stronger after the brick fell.

"What do you make of that?" Stevens asked with a cough. A slimy, vomit streamer dangled from his nose as he remained hunched over his puke. "Does your boy seem like such an innocent man now?"

"I think we need to call in backup. Get an ambulance and let the church know we found something down here."

"You can call. I'll keep working until we can get him out of there." Stevens wiped away the streamer with the back of his hand, than wiped that on his pants.

"Please help me," a voice from inside the brick pillar said just before Martinez pressed the button on his radio to make the call back to the station.

"Hello," Stevens called as he ran to the opening. "Timothy? I'm Officer Stevens; I'm here with Officer Martinez. We're going to get you out. Hold tight."

Martinez, now feeling that he almost let his partner down with his doubts, jumped right in and began wriggling and prying the bricks. The smell of death was still unbearably strong, but the hope of life kept it at bay. One by one the bricks came loose, crunching and grinding painfully like a giant with concrete teeth having a particularly bad molar pulled. They clattered heavily to the floor, covering up the soft sobs of the little boy trapped within.

"I think I have him!" Martinez exclaimed as the opening in the pillar grew with each brick tossed aside.

The top of the boy's head could be seen clearly. The tangled and blood-matted hair fueled a rage in Martinez that he didn't even know was possible. It made him sick to think a father could truly do this to his son.

Stevens rubbed his hands together greedily. This is exactly what he's been waiting for. As soon as this boy was safely out of this church he was going to kick Edwin's front door open and bust his skull. If he ever wanted to see his teeth again he'd have to sift through his shit. *Hope you don't flush 'em,* Stevens rehearsed in his head.

The side of the pillar they had been working on was about halfway down when the blood started trickling over the bricks and running to the floor. It wasn't there before, and it was far too much blood for the small boy to bleed out. Martinez instinctively stopped. Thinking the boy would drown, he reached in and grabbed the boy by his arms, lifting his head above the blood.

With the boy's blood caked face finally clear of the thick pool, his eyes opened. A breathe of smoke rolled out from under each eyelid as they lifted. Behind the smoke, cloudy globes spun restlessly.

"Thank you, mister," the little boy said. His voice was sweet and sincere. The remaining bricks fell free, spilling the blood everywhere and soaking both men's boots. Timothy stepped out of the pillar and stood before them, the image of perfection. He was dressed in his "Sunday Best" with no traces of blood or blemishes on him, despite the widening pool at his feet.

"Oh shit!" Stevens exclaimed and started to run for the stairs as his fight or flight response chose flight in this moment of confusion and dread when it had always chosen to fight in the past. He slipped in the slick blood and went down hard and fast, taking a stray brick to the gut and forcing the air from his lungs. The sound he made was like a low, stupid laugh. *Haaaaaa!*

Martinez was frozen in terror. He stared into the deep red eyes—wax spheres—and his nose started to bleed. Timothy looked back at the officer. His face was calm and almost curious. He stood on top of the blood, which was now several inches deep across the entire basement floor. Stevens sputtered and spit as he lifted himself off his stomach and climbed unsteadily to his knees, his head a jumble.

"Now I can go home to my daddy," Timothy said. Stringy strands of what remained of his torn out tongue flopped about wickedly as he spoke.

For a moment, Martinez started to believe that this was something spiritual. They had freed the boy's soul, now it would dissipate and rest eternally in the Heavenly Kingdom. A tear ran down from his eye, mingling above his lip with the blood running from his nose.

Pain began to build up in his head, like a migraine. Martinez felt like his head would burst if the pain didn't stop. He could hear Stevens shouting for him, but the shouts were a mile away, and the words were all but lost in the distance. A glimmer of lost hope, like a man stranded on an island watching a cruise ship pass by completely unaware of his presence. Lost in the swirl of smoke inside the little boy's eyes, Martinez accepted death.

Hitting the ground hard, Martinez was sure his life had ended horribly, but Stevens' screams snapped him back to the gruesome reality that played out in the basement of that holy place. Stevens had slammed Martinez to the ground, being caught himself in the boy's storming gaze. He tried to climb to his feet and return the favor, to save his partner and friend, but he wasn't quick enough.

Silence enveloped the basement just before Stevens' guts erupted from his stomach with enough force to rip through his uniform and spray what remained of the pillar. Intestines clung to the bricks like strands of Christmas lights. His kidneys and liver splattered like paintballs. Shreds of flesh hung down over the hole in his stomach like moss draped over a cave entrance. The scene played out as if the officer was shot in the back point-blank with a canon.

Stevens dropped to his knees, shocked. His mind raced, and told him not to give up. He picked his stomach up out of the blood with one hand, and grabbed a handful of intestine with the other. Blood poured from his mouth as he tried to stuff his guts back into his body. He picked up squishy slabs of meat and blood covered ropes. He wasn't sure where any of it went, but he pushed it back inside the gaping hole in his stomach. All he had to do was get them back inside and everything would be alright. Then he collapsed.

Martinez pulled the Beretta from its holster and prepared to fire, but the basement had gone dark. There was no sign of the boy, and the blood was gone. The pillar bricks were scattered across the floor. He knelt beside his partner, being careful not to step on any of the dead man's organs, the Beretta still ready to fire at the first sign of the sonofabitch who'd done this.

"This is Officer Martinez requesting back up. I have an officer down. I repeat: I have an officer down! I'm in the basement of the Church of Christ on the corner of Maple and Cherry in Kathrine," Martinez called into his police radio.

VII

June 11th, 3:00 A.M:

Lincoln's night hadn't gone well, but it did go better for him than it did for the two officers who'd gone down into the church's basement. He was hoping to patch things up with Kaydence, but she wasn't in the mood to listen. She did, however, let him sleep inside, shower and eat dinner. Not the chicken shish kabobs and corn on the cob she had made, but he was allowed a microwaved dinner.

Kaydence had told him to sleep on the couch as soon as she opened the door (it felt weird knocking at his own home), and that was the only thing she said to him. Sadie was excited to see him home. She hadn't really remembered much from the other night, and Kaydence, despite her anger toward Lincoln, told their daughter it was just a bad dream.

The couch, as he had learned from many lazy afternoons watching hockey, was pretty damn comfortable. The only part of falling asleep that he would find difficult was not having his wife in his arms. But just being in the house was a huge step forward. Lincoln was positive this would all blow over tomorrow. Plus, for the first time since he started this church job he felt normal.

He didn't even have to work into a comfortable position before sleep took him.

But it didn't last long. Whispering in his head stirred him from that much needed sleep. He awoke feeling as if someone else was in his brain, reading his thoughts like a magazine, watching his memories like old home movies. The language of the strange whisper was old, one he couldn't understand. Maybe it was nothing more than gibberish. He looked around the dark room, expecting to see someone there. Expecting to see the dark figure of the demon, his eyes darted around to the chairs, but the room was empty.

He chose to keep the pastor's story of the demon to himself, as he knew Kaydence would either think him crazy or find it a lame attempt at her forgiveness. There was no other way he could think of to let her know they may be in danger without spurring her to call the police or have him committed to Mireside, at least until after this rough patch he'd found himself in with her had cleared away. He really didn't want to sleep, but he knew he was exhausted and needed the rest, yet there was something pulling at his mind that he couldn't quite ignore.

Lincoln stood and gave his eyes a moment to adjust to the darkness. He walked quietly up the stairs, the feeling that something was terribly wrong started out as a shallow pin prick before escalating to a blaze that wrenched his gut. Everywhere he looked as he reached the top of the stairs he saw shadows move, crawling up the walls and across the ceiling. Lincoln felt that the shadows watched him. Not physically with eyes, but with a sense he couldn't comprehend. The silence enveloping him was almost maddening. Reality felt as if it had slipped away, being pulled from the existence around him by an exhaust fan.

Sadie Elizabeth's bedroom door was open. Lincoln stepped through into what felt like a freezer, leaving behind the comfortable warmth of the hallway. Frost stretched across the inside of the windows in great white patches. The floor was like a sheet of ice across a freezing lake or skating rink. There wasn't even comfort to be found in the rug, as its fibers were frozen, digging into the pads of his feet like little needles. His body begged his brain to turn back, not for fear of the cold or pain from the fiber spikes, something menacing was with him. Something threatening.

Pushing forward, Lincoln made his way further in. On the nightstand by Sadie's bed sat the doll. Surrounded by the cold, the little doll seemed at peace, but there was something eerie about it. Lincoln felt as if it watched him as he crept across the room, not like the shadows in the hall watched him, but like a guard dog.

He couldn't shake the feeling that the doll, Bethesda, the earthly name the demon had taken, needed to be destroyed. Lincoln stood over the doll and reached a shaky hand out to take it. Something in his mind roared as his fingers wrapped around the linen and straw figure.

Destroying the doll would surely destroy the demon. That's where its power is stored. Damn the girl's soul. This is his chance to save his daughter. A nagging voice continued in his head somewhere like peer-pressure.

It's alright. Do it. You wanna be cool, right? Then tear that fucking doll to pieces and light it on fire!

Lincoln reached for the doll, and pain seared in his eyes, ears, and throat, as if he walked into a wall of thick black smoke. Only this was an agony that poured into him, racing for his core and setting his flesh on fire. His skin began to itch, drying and cracking before his eyes. Fear and anger—hatred—consumed him, threatening to turn his body inside out. The veins in his body squirmed and twisted.

Through teary eyes, he saw Sadie standing on her bed. She stood tall, much taller than her size should allow, almost extraterrestrial. Where her nightgown normally covered her ankles it now stopped just above her knees. Her neck stretched up several inches farther than normal, fingers long and branch-like.

His hands, as if working on their own, reached for her. Although her body had grown in some grotesque way, she still seemed fragile. He wanted to hold her tight, to calm her. He wanted to strangle her. The evil seeped from her body, and he wanted to snuff it out.

"You're too late," she said in a voice that was just a cheap imitation of her own. "I have this child's soul."

"You can't have it," Lincoln said in what felt like a scream. He hadn't noticed until now that there was a loud, sustained roar, as if they stood just outside of a tornado. If he hadn't known there were no train tracks close by he would have sworn a freight train barreled past the window. "I'll die saving her soul."

Sadie Elizabeth looked to him with a calm hurt in her eyes. "And you'll have to," she responded.

Lincoln's skin started peeling as the noise grew louder. It itched so bad he couldn't help but scratch at it. The tears in his eyes turned to blood, giving the girl's room a demonic, red hue that Lincoln found appropriate given the circumstances. Pain like he had never imagined engulfed him. He tried to scream, but the noise had become so loud he wasn't sure if it escaped his lips or not.

Eternity came and went before Lincoln finally passed out.

June 11th, 7:05 A.M:

"Hey! Wake up, Lincoln!" Kaydence gave him a sharp kick to the ribs. Obviously, she was still pissed.

Lincoln jolted upright and placed his hands protectively over his stinging side. He was on the floor of Sadie's room. "What time is it?"

"Don't worry, you're not late to work. As a matter of fact I'm waking you up just in time to leave," she said angrily before walking over to wake up Sadie.

"How long are you going to do this?" he asked.

Instead of answering his question, she asked one of her own. She sounded lost in thought. "Lincoln, what the hell is this?"

He sighed, not really in the mood for her shit right now. "What?"

"Oh shit, Lincoln. W—" she couldn't finish her sentence.

Lincoln turned to his daughter's bed as Kaydence pulled the blanket the rest of the way off the girl. They both stared in amazement as Sadie was several inches above the sheets. There was a confusing wave of relief mixed with fear. He wasn't seeing things if she saw this, too.

"Sadie, sweetheart?" Kaydence shook her gently.

The little girl mumbled something, the last remnants of a ponies and rainbows dream. She opened her eyes, and as she did, her body fell to the bed. The fall was quick but startling. Her eyes widened for a second, than she accepted it as just an odd feeling of coming out of sleep. "Good morning, Mommy," she said with a smile as she rubbed the sleep from her eyes.

Kaydence was speechless for half a minute.

"Is everything OK, Mommy?" Sadie asked.

"Run downstairs and I'll get your breakfast started, but don't—" Kaydence started still sounding lost.

"I know, 'don't run down the stairs'," Sadie finished.

As soon as her footsteps faded at the bottom of the

stairs Kaydence said, "What the hell was that? You saw that right?"

"I saw it." Lincoln stood up and walked toward the door, not giving any indications of being surprised by the sight.

"No, you didn't see what I saw, because what I saw isn't possible." Kaydence wore a confused look as she let the possibilities sprint through her mind. "Where the hell are you going?" She stood up and walked toward her husband. Her eyes had been playing tricks on her, that's all.

"I think we need to talk about something," Lincoln said, his lackadaisical expression replaced with concern. "There is something really messed up happening, and I think it may be my fault."

"What are you talking about?" she stood up and charged over to him. "And what happened to your arms?" She reached down and grabbed his left arm, lifting it for a better look.

He didn't need to look to know the scratches were there. After how badly his skin itched last night, he wasn't surprised to see he'd done a number on his arms. "I don't know. I must've gotten into something at the church." He sure as hell wasn't telling her about seeing his skin shred the way it had and scratching away layer after layer, at least not until he's had a chance to fully explain the situation.

She knew that he'd come home before with scratches and bruises from work, and it always made her feel good to take care of him. Instinctually, she pulled him along to the bathroom where she cleaned his cuts. Neither spoke for several minutes, but when Kaydence had finished, she wrapped her arms around him and apologized.

Then she started laughing. Slowly at first, but her laughter built up until tears ran down her cheeks.

"What's so funny," he said, looking down into her brown eyes as they glistened back at him through her tears.

"I could've sworn that Sadie was floating over her bed this morning. That must make me sound insane. I mean, I could actually see the gap between her and her sheets."

Lincoln took this as a sign that he should keep his mouth shut, at least for now. "It's just been a rough couple of days," he said. He knew she needed to know about this demon, if the demon was real and *he* wasn't insane, but he also had hope that he could stop it before she had to know.

She nodded and said, "I better get Sadie her breakfast. French toast this morning. Why don't you go in a little late this morning and have breakfast with us?"

"Sounds fantastic, but I really should be going. I need to check on the bricks I put up last night. I'll leave work early and come home for lunch instead." He smiled and kissed her forehead softly.

"Oh, did you want to tell me something a little bit ago?" Kaydence asked.

"I can't remember what it was now. Must not have been important." He felt as if he'd just dodged a bullet, but he knew it would come back around like a boomerang.

The doorbell rang, causing Lincoln to jump. Kaydence chuckled a little at this and walked out into the hallway. He followed her downstairs, where his phone rang on the stand next to the couch in the family room. It was set to vibrate, so it chattered loudly against the wood surface.

"Hello," he said as he held it to his ear.

"Lincoln, this is Pastor Simmons. It seems you can take the next few days off. I hope that doesn't get in the way of the next job you have lined up. I certainly don't mean to cause a scheduling conflict, but there was a terrible accident last night and the basement is blocked off. An officer was . . . well, an officer was killed down there."

"Oh God," Lincoln said. He felt awful, made even worse when he realized his biggest concern was that his work had collapsed and killed someone more than the fact that someone had died. "Yeah. Hey, can I still stop by today? I need to talk to you."

"Of course, Lincoln. You are encouraged to come to the house of God anytime you need Him." Lincoln found it strange the way the pastor stretched out the word, *Gaawd*, like it left a bad taste in his mouth.

"Thank you. I'll see you shortly after lunch?"

"That will be just perfect, Lincoln."

"Great. Thank you."

Lincoln hung up without waiting for a goodbye from the other end. He tossed the phone down onto the couch and looked up to see who was at the door.

"Good morning, Lincoln. I hope me stopping by isn't too much of an intrusion. I snagged your info from the side of your truck and looked your address up in the phonebook." Edwin stood just inside the entryway, looking like he had a rougher night than Lincoln had.

"They still make phonebooks?" Lincoln couldn't remember when the last time he'd received one was. "But yeah, come on in. It's not a problem at all," Lincoln said with a genuine smile. He turned to Kaydence. "I'll be staying for breakfast after all. French toast sounds great."

This made her smile, and she wore it beautifully. "Would you like some French toast, coffee?" She looked to Edwin.

"Coffee would be fantastic," Edwin responded. If anyone looked as if they needed coffee, it was Edwin. His short hair was standing straight up in some spots, his skin was flushed, and there were dark bags under his eyes.

"So what brings you out here?" Lincoln asked as they walked to the kitchen. He gestured for Edwin to have a seat at a barstool in front of the island.

Edwin saw the little girl sitting at the table in the breakfast nook and decided he didn't want to frighten her or Lincoln's wife. "Actually, can we have just a minute?"

"Sure. That gives us time for this coffee to cool, anyway," Lincoln said with a friendly grin. He led the way through the family room and out into the garage. Pegboards lined the walls with perfectly placed tools hung neatly. A large red toolbox sat in the corner next to a large air compressor. A 34 Ford Coupe sat in the far bay. "What's up?"

"I assume the phone call you got as I showed up was from the church?" Edwin admired the lime green hot rod. The hood and fenders had been removed, exposing the 302 small-block power plant.

Lincoln only nodded that it was.

"Well the police officers that went down there were the same guys who stopped by while you were over. Cory Stevens is the name of the man who was killed down there."

"I'm sorry to hear that." Lincoln remembered Edwin saying that Cory Stevens was kind of a dick but felt confident that he was a genuinely good man. "The other officer, he's alright?"

"Well he's alive. I watched them come up. It was a real circus. I thought the gawkers were bad when my boy went missing." His eyes seemed to trail off in thought. "Anyway, I really want you to be careful when you go back to work down there. I don't think his death was an accident, and it sure as hell isn't a coincidence that all of this started happening when you started working down there," he said before quickly adding, "I'm not blaming you, though. None of this is your fault."

"I appreciate that, but it's just a hell of a thing to think that maybe I let this damn thing out. We wouldn't be asshole deep in whatever this is." Lincoln was really beginning to feel that this man's son's blood was on his hands.

"Whatever the hell this *is*, I don't think you let it out. I got a creepy vibe from that church last night watching them carry that officer out of the basement on a stretcher. And I don't mean that vibe you get from seeing a dead body. I mean I felt like there was something *wrong* with that church. Like the holiness has been drained and replaced with a stygian darkness."

"I think you need to know something." Lincoln inhaled deeply and paused for several seconds before exhaling in a loud huff. "You *deserve* to know something. When I first started working in the basement I found a box. It was in a brick pillar that I thought at first was a support structure. I now think it was a tomb built for that box." The way the last sentence left his lips sent shivers down his spine and caused goosebumps to rise on Edwin's arms. "This box had a strange symbol on it, a circle with a cross and a black rock, onyx as it turns out, and a silver star.

"Inside that box was a doll." Lincoln sat on one of the

fat tires sticking out from the back of the Coupe and told Edwin all about the Order of Onyx and Light, Jesus' battle with this demon, losing the girl, and how their souls were trapped together in the doll. Edwin listened contently as Lincoln told the story while Lincoln watched Edwin, waiting for him to laugh and walk away. He doubted he would, as Edwin had definitely seen some crazy shit, too.

Neither man consciously noticed the temperature dropping in the garage as Lincoln continued with his story despite both men rubbing the chill from their arms on several occasions. The neatly arranged tools hanging from the pegboard walls began to vibrate, the windows throughout the entire house rattled, but just softly enough to go unnoticed.

"And now the demon—merged with the soul of that little girl—is out of its tomb."

The water in the kitchen sink, as well as those in both the downstairs, and upstairs bathrooms, began to drip, slowly speeding up to a trickle.

"Do you know what the demon's name is?" asked Edwin who was feeling more and more uncomfortable as the seconds ticked away. "Maybe we can look it up. There's all kinds of crazy shit on the internet. I'm sure someone has a blog or something telling us how to kill all sorts of demons."

"I don't know what its name *was*, but since merging with the girl inside the doll, it's taken on the dolls name. Like it's a new being now, or it's mocking the girl by taking on the name of something she loved." Lincoln was almost positive he felt something in his feet. A tingling like his feet were falling asleep.

The tools continued to vibrate faster until the soft pulse could be felt in the air.

"So what's its name now?" Edwin sounded almost annoyed that he had to ask. Lincoln should have just come out and said it. The vibrating hum tickled the thin hairs in Edwin's ears, but Lincoln's tale had consumed his senses to the point where nothing else mattered. He could be standing in fire and still had to hear the end of the story before he noticed.

"Bethesda."

All at once the tools fell from the wall in a chaotic clanging of chrome-plated steel that was barely audible over the sounds of the windows shattering. Glass crashed to the floor and the house vibrated so hard and so fast that it actually let out a hum that could be heard for miles but would go relatively unnoticed. The trickle of water from the faucets turned to waterfalls of boiling water with steam gushing up like smoke from a volcano. Lincoln heard Kaydence scream, and he ran past Edwin, trying to keep his balance on the quaking floor.

"What's happening?" she screamed as she saw the two men run into the house. Sadie lay in her arms. Her little body convulsed and twisted while foam boiled up from her mouth and ran down her cheeks, through her long hair, and eventually spread across the trembling tile floor.

"I don't know. We need to get her to the hospital!" Lincoln yelled as he took her in his arms. The cupboards shook open, spilling plates, bowls, and glasses.

"I'll get the door!" Edwin shouted over the loud humming and shattering glass. He ran ahead, wrapped his right hand around the shaking doorknob and pulled. The vibrations stopped. The water did, too. Everything was quiet except for Kaydence's frightened sobs.

"Is everything alright here, folks?"

Edwin swallowed hard and looked at the second most terrifying smile he'd ever seen. The first was worn by the vision of his son in the holding cell. This one, by the man who'd put him there in the first place.

"Alex," Edwin said. His heart beat so hard he could feel it against his chest. "It's a surprise to see you here. We actually have a sick kid we were getting ready to take to the hospital, so if you don't mind—"

"It's Officer Martinez, and I really do mind. It seems like more of a surprise to me . . . that I would see *you* here." His crazed glare went from Edwin to Lincoln. The officer swayed slightly and reeked of booze. "It seems that there has been a tragic accident." He used his fingers to make quotes in the air as he said accident.

"We heard," Lincoln spoke up. "I'm very sorry to hear

that. I'm sure he was—"

"Shut your fucking mouth right now! You don't know shit about him. He was a better man than you'll ever be. He risked his life for this country; he would have risked his life for you and your son." He pointed at Edwin. "And as soon as I can prove you two had something to do with his death, I'm coming back here." He unholstered his gun and pointed it loosely back and forth between the two men. "And I'm going to blow both of your fucking brains out. I trusted you, Edwin. I really thought you were a good man in a bad situation."

"Whoa now. We had nothing to do with any of this," Lincoln protested. "Please. I just want to get my daughter to the hospital." He held her up a little higher as if to say see.

"How do I know that you didn't poison her? Is that what you did to little Timothy? I'm going to catch you, and when I do." He pointed his gun at all three of them this time and looked around. "I can't believe you live in this shithole. Broken glass everywhere; seems like a dangerous environment for a child. I should come back here with protective services and take that girl away from you. As a matter of fact, I'll have them meet you at the hospital."

"That's fine; just get out of the way so we can get there." Lincoln stepped past the officer and ran for Kaydence's car. He buckled the girl into the back seat of the white Dodge Dart and ran to the driver's side. Kaydence hopped in the passenger's side, and Edwin ran for his Mercedes-Benz C350, which was the only thing Karen left with him besides their son. Before climbing in, he looked back to the man he once thought could end up being a friend, but Martinez had become unstable, and Edwin hoped after a good night's sleep and a few days off he'd get his health back.

Officer Martinez stood on the porch and watched the family leave, followed by Mr. Carmichael. He wanted to follow them, make sure they didn't take that little girl somewhere and leave her for dead, but he didn't care if they did. Fuck her, anyway. She was nothing but another body for the list of shit he was going to nail them for.

The sound of glass crunching in the house behind him caused Martinez to turn. He gave a listen for the cars, but they were long gone. He stepped into the house and looked around at the mess. *What the hell happened in here*, he thought. The glass from the windows had dropped straight down as if it had shattered on its own rather than being busted in or out.

Shards of glass and porcelain were layered across the kitchen floor. Air bubbles escaped a puddle of white foam where the little girl must've collapsed after she was poisoned. The crunching came from behind him, and he turned around to find himself face to gruesome face with Stevens. The sight of him was grotesque. His shirt was soaked in blood, and it was open enough to see the hole that had been busted open in his stomach. Martinez wanted to tell his partner that he looked like shit, but the words weren't there.

A warm stream of piss ran down Martinez' leg, soaking his pants and pooling in his shoe. But he didn't feel fear. Instead, he felt love and comfort. He looked into the secluded sorrow of his partner's face. He wanted to say something, but the words continued to stick in his throat.

"Alex," Stevens whispered. Although his mouth moved in perfect synchronization with the word, the sound didn't come from his lips. Martinez wasn't sure if it came from everywhere at once or was just in his head.

"You're dead," Martinez finally said. His throat was scratchy, and he had to force the words. "I saw you die." He pointed to his partner's stomach.

"Yeah. I am," Stevens responded. His gloomy, lifeless—yet strangely caring—eyes told Martinez the truth. It was truth of a thousand ages.

"You saved me, and I couldn't do anything for you. It should be me that's dead!" Martinez exclaimed. His voice came off a bit confused. "I was terrified, and I couldn't react fast enough."

"It isn't your fault, Alex." He placed a cold hand on Martinez' shoulder and squeezed gently. "But in order to really nail the bastards that killed me, everything needs to go off just right." Stevens said, his expression never changing. His tone was flat, dark, and filled with love all at once.

Martinez nodded his understanding. Than shook his head in confusion. "But who killed you?"

"Edwin and Lincoln did." Stevens responded. A thick streamer of blood leaked from his mouth.

"They weren't there, Cory. I couldn't even find the body of Edwin's son after what happened."

"That's because they set us up, Alex. They set us up to kill us. We were too close to finding out the truth, so they killed me, almost killed you. While you were trying to call in help for me, they took the boy and ran. Now, Alex. You really need to listen to what I have to tell you. There are powerful forces at work. You need to choose which side you want to be on," Stevens said.

"I'm on your side." There was no hesitation in Martinez' words.

"Good. I really need you to trust me, Alex. I wish there was a better way to end this, a simpler way, but there must be sacrifices. Lincoln may have to die, Alex. Do you understand?"

Martinez nodded obediently.

"Now, this is what you have to do." Stevens didn't say anything after that, but Martinez could see what he wanted from him. A simple plan was laid out before Martinez as if he were watching a slide show. He liked it, but there was certainly room for improvement. His first change to his partner's plan; he had to take a few things, just some personal items that may come in handy soon. There was also a doll that lay on the bed in the girl's room. It had to be taken somewhere safe for now, until the time came when it would be needed again.

VIII

June 11th, 10:41 A.M:

"Well, she does have a bump on her head, but other than that she seems fine," Doctor Hartley said after examining Sadie. "The tests we ran show no signs of any abnormalities, her vitals are strong. Perhaps she's developed an allergy, so check your house for anything new you may have brought into the home recently. Perhaps you've changed something like laundry detergents. If you want we can do allergy testing, but other than that I'd say this little girl is ready to roll." She smiled down at the girl and patted her knee.

"Thanks," Kaydence replied before helping her daughter down from the exam table. She and Lincoln had brought Sadie straight to the hospital, deciding to worry about whatever the hell had happened at home when they got back.

"Just keep an eye on her over the next few days and bring her ASAP if, and that's a pretty big IF, this happens again," Doctor Hartley advised.

As a med student at the University of Iowa, Doctor Hartley was doing rounds in Labor and Delivery when Sadie was born. Although her shift had ended, she stuck around for another hour and talked to Lincoln and Kaydence, helping them with everything they needed. Her blue-gray eyes had a stern yet caring feel that they both found comforting. As soon as they found out she had become a pediatrician a year later, they brought Sadie to see her.

Lincoln led the way down the hall. Sadie had perked up since arriving at the hospital, and she held her mom's hand as she skipped along beside her. As they drew closer to the front desk, Lincoln saw a man standing (*like a smear,* Lincoln thought) against the wall. His eyes lingered on the family too long to just be a passing glance.

"Mr. and Mrs. Scott?" he asked in a strict, unfriendly voice that said this man was all business.

"Yes," Lincoln said with a little hesitation. *A smear that keeps getting worse the more you try to clean it.*

"I need you to walk with me, please." Without waiting for an answer, the smear of a man peeled away from the wall and walked ahead of Lincoln and out through the large sliding doors.

"You don't think this has to do with that cop from this morning do you?" Kaydence asked. A lump formed in her throat and her stomach knotted, but she swallowed her fear and tried to look calm.

"Unfortunately, I do."

As they stepped out into the bright summer sun, they saw officer Martinez—slightly more sober—standing by the Dart. He just grinned and nodded. Beside him was another officer. This man, the silver nameplate on his uniform read Sgt. Williams, was a full nine inches taller than Martinez, his well-defined muscle wrapped in light-ebony skin.

"Is there a problem?" Lincoln said as they walked up to their car.

"I'm Mark Hoover of Child Protective Services," the smear said. "Officer Martinez has brought us photographic evidence that suggests your home may not be fit for a child to live in." Mr. Hoover brushed his black hair back with his hand. His suit seemed just a little too short in the arms. He smelled of cheap cologne, or maybe it was Martinez covering up the alcohol.

Lincoln looked between him and the two officers. Sgt. Williams clearly outranked Martinez, and didn't seem all too pleased that he was dragged out here for this. Domestic disputes were beneath him at this point in his career, but he didn't like what he sensed was going on with Martinez, so he decided it best be here.

"Did Officer Martinez also tell you that he showed up to my house this morning drunk and waving a gun around? If you take my daughter on this man's word, then I want him to pass a breathalyzer right now. Look at him! I think he's still drunk." Lincoln leaned toward him and sniffed the air. "He smells of beer and what I'm pretty sure is piss."

Lincoln hoped like hell that the officers couldn't hear the fear in his words. His heart pounded so hard he thought it would burst, but he continued talking. "His uniform is a wreck. Did he sleep in a dumpster last night? I'm sorry to hear of the death of this man's partner, and I'm concerned as to why he wasn't given a few days off to get himself in order. If we're done here, gentleman, I have to get home and clean up. Some punk kids, or drunken police officers, showed up this morning and busted out every one of my windows."

Lincoln signaled for Kaydence to get Sadie in the car and started walking around to the driver's side. He could feel the cockiness in his step. That came out damn smooth and he was quite impressed with himself.

Officer Martinez made a move to stop him, but was held back by Sgt. Williams, who certainly recognized the same smells that Lincoln had. The much larger man placed his hand on Steven's chest and shook his head. From the look he gave Martinez, Lincoln new the officer was in deep shit.

Mr. Hoover wasn't even sure how to handle this situation. He fumbled in his blazer pocket for his phone. "Mr. Scott," Mr. Hoover said as he brought his phone to his ear. "I think it'll be appropriate to give you a couple days to take care of your property. We'll be stopping by to check on your progress. Thank you for your time, and I hope your daughter gets to feeling better soon." He turned around as he began talking into his phone.

"Thanks guys," Lincoln said with a smile. He waved before ducking down into the driver's seat of the car.

Officer Martinez watched as the car pulled out of the parking lot. That hadn't gone exactly as he'd planned, if he'd been the one to plan it, which he was sure he had. But he was confident that this was the way it must have to go. Everything would work itself out. The child had to be taken away. In order for this all to work, the little girl had to be separated from her father.

June 11th, 4:15 P.M:

Lincoln was amazed that he could get an insurance agent out to his house on such short notice. They always seemed friendly and right there when needed on the commercials (just do the jingle), but he assumed in real life they'd be a pain in the ass. The agent was a short, goofy looking man, but he was friendly and insisted on being called Greg.

After Greg took a few pictures, a ton of notes, and made a few phone calls, he had an estimate of what the insurance would pay. He could see the urgency in the situation, so he promised them a check in the morning after he pushed the paperwork through the system as quick as he could. To Lincoln's amazement, the entire process only took two hours.

An hour after Greg set out on a return trip to his home office Lincoln had swept all the glass off the floor. He'd worked on it alone while Kaydence took Sadie out to play on the swing in the backyard. The small fragments of glass scraped and clattered as they were pushed across the floor by the soft bristles of the broom.

Underneath the scrapes and clatters, however, Lincoln heard something else. He stopped and listened, but the sound vanished, stopping dead in its tracks as if it'd hit a barrier. Another long sweep and the sound returned, and this time he could hear it. It was the voice heard in a wind chime by an imaginative child if that wind chime just happened to be made of broken glass.

She has to die.

He stopped again and looked around to make sure Kaydence wasn't messing with him. Looking past the stairway, he could just make out his wife and daughter deep in the backyard playing in the small playset with its swings and slides. He strained to hear them, but he couldn't even hear the metallic squeal of the swing through the open window. He shrugged and pushed the thick bristles of the broom across the floor.

I have chosen you, Lincoln.

But Lincoln kept working. Whatever it was he was hearing could talk itself blue. He had an entire house worth of broken windows to clean up. It was certainly a frightening thing to hear, but he was tired, and hearing voices was the least of the frightening things that's happened to him this week. With each new pile he swept, the voice strengthened as if it were being charged by his movement.

You can rule by my side, Lincoln.

Lincoln ignored the voice and swept. It did, however, become harder to push aside. There was beauty in the voice. Whether it was male or female, Lincoln didn't know, but it was seductive in a way that made Lincoln feel it could have loved him deeply, and he could have loved it.

He watched out the window in the small bedroom between Sadie's room and the bathroom. They used it as a spare when family visited, but for now it was storage. The last bit of glass was on the floor, waiting to be swept into the dustpan and dropped into the cardboard box Lincoln was carrying around with him.

The voice continued to speak to him the entire time, but as he swept the last remnants of this strange, possibly demonic event, from the floor, the voice was gone. He dumped the glass in the box. It tinkled and tattered its crystalline song. Dozens of voices coming together like a magnificent Broadway musical.

As the glass shards fell from the dustpan it slowed down, falling in slow motion. Lincoln wanted to believe it was his eyes playing tricks, but too much had happened for him to not believe this demon was real and powerful.

He peeked out the window briefly and saw that his wife and daughter were still playing and doing so at regular speed. Looking back to the falling glass shards he couldn't believe that they were indeed falling far too slow to be real, but it only lasted for a moment before the shards drove down into the box of glass so hard it sounded like a crystal chandelier had fallen in a mansion.

LINCOLN!!

The voice boomed, and the room was filled with the smell of motor oil. The broken glass erupted from the box and spun in the air until it formed the humanoid shape of the demon. Lincoln was stunned by its beauty. A figure made entire of broken glass. Every single inch of the demon was a sharp edge.

Lincoln looked into the glass face of the demon and watched as the glass shards melted into a smooth liquid, turned black, and formed what appeared to be a suit of armor. A long black cloak draped down the back of its mighty form. The rolling eyes of smoke in its head fixed on Lincoln, who stared back just as intently. Up close, the demon's armored physique had a charcoal-esque appearance rather than the smooth appearance Lincoln expected from the melted glass.

Signals raced from Lincoln's brain to every corner of his body telling him the scream, to run away from what he was seeing, but these signals never made it, instead his body received a different signal. This signal came from the demon, and it soothed him and told him everything would be alright.

"Bethesda?" he asked, his voice a dry whisper.

The demon's cloak ruffled as if blown by a sharp gust of wind, and then the creature shattered, leaving glass shards all over the floor in the middle of the room.

Lincoln continued to stare at the scattered glass pile that remained where Bethesda had just been. He felt his bones aching and tiredness seeped into his body and mind almost as if he awoke one morning to the realization that his youth had slipped away. Something wet touched his chest, and when he looked down, he noticed he'd been drooling down the front of his shirt.

It took him a minute to snap fully back to reality, and he quickly cleaned the glass up once again before returning to watching his family out the window despite the feeling that his mind had been pulled in two. There was the unnatural feeling of someone else being inside his head, and although he still wanted to scream, this other mind continued to pacify.

Fifteen minutes later, Lincoln walked back in from the garage, where he'd placed two full boxes of broken glass next to his blue garbage can. After cleaning the glass, and the mess from all the dishes, Lincoln brought in a few rolls of plastic and covered the windows, which gave the natural light a lifeless feel.

"It isn't the best, but it should at least keep any critters out," he said with an amused tone. "I'm really not looking forward to putting all my tools back up."

"Why don't you go upstairs and read, honey," Kaydence said to Sadie just as the little girl plopped down on the couch. She was worn out from playing outside, but she smiled and went upstairs to grab a book.

"What's the matter?" Lincoln asked when he heard Sadie's footsteps in her room.

"*What's the matter*?" Kaydence snapped. "I've kept my cool for Sadie's sake, but what the *fuck* happened this morning?"

"I don't know," he lied. "A strange air pressure fluctuation?"

"Bullshit. Bull—shit. You know more than your saying, Link. And if you don't tell me what's going on I'm going to beat it out of you, and this time I won't hold back."

"You were holding back last time?"

Kaydence glared at him, daring him to keep it up.

"Fine, but you're not going to like this." He knew she deserved to know, and at this point there wasn't any chance of hiding it any longer. He told her all about the demon, the little girl, the doll, Edwin and his son.

Kaydence cried until she broke out into a half-crazed laughter. "So our little girl may be possessed."

"I'm not saying that."

"We need to call a fucking exorcist? The Vatican?" Kaydence looked like her mind would snap at any second as she paced around the room.

"I don't know what we need to do." Lincoln watched her from his perch on the arm of the couch. He didn't want to find out if she'd run him over if he stepped in her way.

"Why don't you talk to the preacher, or whatever he is, at the church? He'll know what to do, right? Right?" Kaydence looked to him with pleading eyes.

"I don't know if he will. Pastor Simmons—" He really didn't know how he felt about the pastor. He sensed something weird with him the last time they spoke, but maybe it was just the stress of this demon being out. Lincoln almost smiled at how easily the thoughts of a demon came to him. It no longer sounded the least bit nuts. "I'll talk to him. If he doesn't know what to do, then he'll surely know who to talk to."

Kaydence nodded dully, then her eyes squinted and her head cocked slightly to the left. "Are you feeling alright?" she asked.

"I'm a bit tired, but other than that." Lincoln gave a shrug that said he was fine.

"You don't look well." Kaydence caressed his face with her fingers. They felt hot against his skin. "You're cold. Maybe you should lie down."

"Actually I want to shower. I feel like I haven't in quite a while. Then I'll call the pastor." He kissed her lips and walked up the stairs to the bathroom. Took a towel from the closet and started the water.

While Lincoln waited for the water to heat up, he examined his naked body in the mirror on the closet door. His skin did seem to be a little flushed, yellow actually, but what really caught his attention wasn't the yellowing of his skin, but how his skin sagged the way an old man's would. The muscle definition was there, but so were stretch marks. White streaks ran in broken trails up his arms, legs, and across the loose flesh on his stomach.

He leaned close to the mirror and pried his eyes open with the index finger and thumb on each hand. Red veins lightning-bolted across the yellowing whites. The pupils dilated as he focused in on them up close rather than constricting. For a second he swore there was someone else deep in the black discs that looked back at him: a curious onlooker peering through a window.

Lincoln hadn't realized how long he stood there until he wiped the moisture from the glass. He turned around and glared through the thick steam that fogged the bathroom. The continuous sound of the shower head raining down its high pressure stream onto the tub floor was disrupted, becoming a gentle patter against soft flesh.

As Lincoln cut through the thick haze he saw the feminine silhouette in the frosted glass of the shower door. He couldn't help but smile. Kaydence could be pretty light on her feet when she wanted to be. It's been too long since their last shower together. The silhouette turned and pressed supple breasts against the glass.

The tingling in his balls caused them to tighten up,

snuggling into the warmth between his legs. He may have started looking like an old man, but he was about to prove he was far from it. His fingertips touched the warm metal frame of the shower door. It glided open smoothly. A rush of warm moisture greeted him, stroking his body provocatively. He inhaled the steam; it felt great in his lungs.

The smell, however, was enough to make him retch. Rotting meat and spoiled milk was how he would've described it, if he'd ever wanted to tell the story to anyone. He'd never kept anything from his wife, but this is something he planned to take to the grave.

The woman in the shower wasn't his wife. He doubted it was a woman he'd ever even seen before. Her skin was split open in some spots and saggy, far worse than his was, and she looked as if she'd been in the shower far too long. Perhaps she'd been at the bottom of a lake for a while. The color of her flesh wasn't one he could even identify: A greenish-purple? Maybe grayish-red? Her face may have been beautiful at one time, perhaps years ago, before she died.

Her long hair was blonde with a seaweed green hue and hung down to her lower back. Clumps of slimy mildew sucked in the shower water in long-awaited drinks. She smiled at him, showing her blackened teeth. Her tongue was bloated and purple. Her hand came up to his face. She caressed his cheek with the back of her bony fingers. He could feel that her fingernails must have fallen out many years ago.

His senses screamed. He wanted out, to have no part of this. Despite his disgust, he could still feel his body's arousal. Only it was no longer his body, he was just along for the ride. Something else had hopped in the driver's seat. The wretched creature before him waited for whatever the wretched creature within him had planned.

He tried to fight, to take his body back, but failed. His hands gripped her, embracing her and pulling her in. Her flesh felt like warm, raw hamburger that had been sitting out on the counter, forgotten overnight. They kissed. He winced. Her tongue entered his mouth, squirming about like a bullfrog fresh out of the swamp, tasted that way, too. Everything in his stomach came up, flooding into both of their mouths, something that seemed to turn her on that much more.

Wrapping her right leg around his waist she thrust her hips toward him. He felt a fresh surge of disgust pierce through his mind like a small caliber bullet as he slid inside her. It was cold and wet. Vomit clung to his chest and dripped from her mouth as she leaned in for another long kiss. He tried to drift off, allowing his mind to roam free as his body thrust into hers, but this demon inside him held him firm. He could hear the laughter from this ancient beast roaring in his head. He felt as if he'd been strapped down and forced to watch this horror unfold before him.

But within the horror show was something profoundly exhilarating. Revulsion and ecstasy danced together in the fluid personification of rapture that ended in a climax that could shatter worlds if it had escaped the confines of Lincoln's bathtub. Pleasure enveloped him in the warmth and safety of its breast while at the same time trying to tear him limb from limb as if he were being pulled apart by Lust herself.

As it finally ended, he collapsed in a heap on the floor of the shower, hot water beating down on him. His entire body shook as the last fragments of pleasure worked its way from every pore. The only remnants of what had happened were a thick carpet of slime and algae and an otherworldly laugh that rang through his head. Regaining control of his body and senses, he used a rag to scrub every sinful yet euphoric detail of his experience clean. After he was finished, he dried off and dressed, but he couldn't fight the thought of climbing back in the shower with Kaydence's hair drier and ending his life. Somehow he knew the demon wouldn't allow that.

Not yet.

June 11th, 9:20 P.M:

Lit by the moon's soft light, Officer Martinez stood in the Hastings Salvage Yard four miles south of Kathrine in the slightly larger town of Gale. The air was filled with the smells of dirt, oil, and a smell Martinez would proudly have described as hard work. On top of that was the lingering smell of diesel exhaust from the old Case twenty ton excavator that sat next to a large pile of steel scrap. On the end of its large boom was a shear attachment that made the whole thing look like a giant one-armed lobster. A large, terrible claw that snapped large hunks of steel like twigs protruded from the single skeletal arm.

Moving past, he worked his way further in to examine rows upon rows of cars, trucks, and vans, long since retired. Each row ran a hundred yards with a path down each isle large enough for the Case excavator to clank and rumble down through on its metal tracks. Fifteen rows made up the large lot.

Every type of car he could imagine was here. Old rust buckets praying to the car gods that someone would come along and ask for just one part from their decaying carcasses, to newer autos, totaled after accidents and dropped off here to be forgotten. He had his pick of the litter.

Stevens had stayed behind, despite being asked several times to come along. Good old fashioned police work, as a team, Martinez had said to him, but Stevens declined, saying he had other business to handle, and he couldn't be seen right now anyway. Everyone else thought—knew—he was dead.

"Besides," Stevens urged, "You won't tell me what you have planned, but I can see in your eyes that it may not be the right way to achieve our goals. Something more subtle is required."

Martinez couldn't help feeling a little like the roles had switched between his partner and him. He couldn't help but think Stevens had become somewhat of a pussy. Sure, something more subtle would be fine, but being betrayed by Edwin (as well as his own intuition) had his blood boiling. He knew what must be done.

Martinez walked slowly through this car cemetery. All makes and models. Take your pick and drive it off the lot today! Only none of these were driving anywhere anytime soon. He didn't need a car that moved. All he needed was a trunk that opened. His plan involved hiding a few bodies and placing someone in the frame. He knew that Edwin and that contractor were murdering sonsabitches who've betrayed his trust, and he planned on killing two birds with one stone, or at least bashing in the brains of a mother and daughter with a stone and pinning it on Edwin and his murderous friend.

Sure there was a flaw in the logic behind his plan, or maybe more like a total fucking misfire, but he was aware of it, and Martinez accepted that there were certain circumstances that required death to stop more death. A virgin sacrifice once a year so the crops grow, feeding the village and keeping everyone else alive, wasn't so crazy. The untimely death of a mother and daughter to put a stop to a couple of guys that will potentially murder a dozen or more works just the same.

Of course, there was no way in Hell that Martinez was going to tell this plan to Stevens. Not *this* plan. Knowing Stevens as well as he did, he knew that his partner would try to talk him into a less destructive course of action. Besides, Stevens seemed a bit off to Martinez. It was almost as if the man wasn't all there anymore. Martinez knew that his plan would come out sooner or later, and when it did, Stevens would see it was the right way to go about accomplishing what they set out to do.

For now, what he needed was enough evidence to lock those two up for good. Plus, there was the added bonus of child murderers getting it pretty rough in prison.

"Can I help you find something?" A voice from behind Officer Martinez came from out of nowhere. It was stern with a hint of yeah-we're-closed-and-it's-dark-as-hell-but-I'll-sell-you-whatever-you-want-if-you're-paying-cash.

Martinez turned around and put on the friendliest smile he could muster. It made him look batshit crazy. Or maybe it was the fact that he *was* batshit crazy that made him look that way. Either way, he stared into the face of a middle aged man. Despite the late hour, he was well dressed. Stevens assumed he had probably changed out of his PJs when he noticed a man on his property. His white t-shirt was tucked neatly into his faded blue jeans. The large buckle on his belt shined in the dim moonlight, and his cowboy boots kicked up puffs of dust with each heavy step.

"Oh! Hello, officer. Is there a problem?" There was a hint of concern in the man's voice. "If you're looking for something from the cars that come from the police impound they are back in the south-east corner, unless you're looking for something else, of course."

"No, actually we were pursuing a hit and run suspect when he ditched his vehicle and took off on foot." Martinez' eyes narrowed as he looked around, waiting for the first sign of movement in the shadowy spaces between the cars. "I'm sure he's long gone. Just a drunk kid on the run, he's not dangerous, though. It was a parked car he hit. I'll be getting out of here, sir. I hope I didn't frighten you and your family with my intrusion."

"No, not at all. I appreciate what you guys do, you know? Police officers are real heroes. Name's Brian Hastings, by the way." The middle aged man, who had owned this salvage yard since his father passed away decades ago, gave a friendly nod. "Do you need help finding your way out? You're also welcome to continue your search in here if you feel the young man may still be running around. I doubt he'll be any real trouble, though. I remember causing quite the ruckus back in my youth." His laugh was warm and friendly.

"I'm sure he's long gone by now. Fast on his feet, for sure. He was really hauling ass," Martinez said. He answered Mr. Hastings' laughed with one of his own that came out shrill and nervous. "Hey, is that a Roadrunner under there?"

"Oh, it's actually a Satellite. You a Mopar guy?" The man stepped a little closer to the officer.

"Yeah. I actually purchased a Roadrunner last week. Cali car. Should be delivered in the next few days. In great shape, but I wouldn't mind having some extra parts, just in case."

The man knelt down in front of the Satellite, but never had a chance to speak. If he had, he would have told the officer that he would pull the ol' car out and have it hauled his way, free of charge for his dedicated service, first thing in the morning. Instead, a strong force drove his forehead down onto the rusted trunk lid. The impact dented the car and caused fracturing in Brian's frontal bone.

He plopped down on his ass in the dry dirt and tried to look up. He wanted to look to help, hoping that a rogue gust of wind, or that damned drunk, had knocked him over. Instead, he looked through blurry eyes at the officer standing above him. It must have been a mistake. He lifted his hands and mouthed the words, help me.

In the dark he couldn't make out the face of the officer standing above him, but if he could he would have seen both fear and deranged desire in the man's wide eyes. What he did see, however, was the officer raise his right foot, and in the course of a second, the blackness grew, engulfing his vision as the hard soul of the officer's boot sped up on a crash course with Brian's face. His head was stuck between a rock and a hard place. In this case, it was the bumper of a 72 Plymouth Satellite and a heavy work boot that seemed a little too large for the foot inside.

The collision broke the cartilage in his nose, shattered the nasal bone, and knocked out his front teeth. The back of his head split open, spewing warm blood down the back of his neck in spurts. Brian tried to raise his arms, this time in self-defense, but neither arm would listen. They just lay there at his side. He couldn't even look at the officer. One eye had shut down completely while the other jerked in its socket wildly. All he could do was await the next blow. The killing blow.

And it came swiftly.

The warm body twitched at his feet while the blood pooled on the ground. Officer Martinez felt the rage build in him. The murdering had to stop. He couldn't allow those two to go free for much longer, or the body count would surely keep rising.

He snapped on a pair of latex gloves, than another to reduce his fingerprints even further. It took some work, but the trunk of the Satellite popped open. Martinez pressed on the floor firmly, seemed solid enough. His body was growing weak, either from lack of sleep or he was coming down with something. He hadn't been feeling entirely himself, after all. It took a little work, but he was able to slide the body in and tuck it against the backside of the seats that made up the front wall of the trunk.

From his front pants pocket he pulled a freezer bag. Inside that bag were several smaller bags. He grabbed a bag with a number one written on it in marker and extracted a few strands of brown hair from a comb in Lincoln's bathroom. He tucked them into Mr. Hastings' fist. Martinez than plowed the blood clumped dirt far under the rusted car with the boots he wore and swept in dirt from the path he had walked down to replace what he'd pushed back. He admired his ability to make it look as though nobody had been here. He didn't want someone stumbling on the crime scene until it was complete.

After deciding that nothing really looked out of place, even to a police officer, he made his way out of the salvage yard. What used to be a cemetery for old autos was now the temporary resting place for the unfortunate owner. It was almost too perfect that he would show up at all.

Before Martinez climbed into his cruiser he untied Lincoln's bloody boots and stuffed them into a plastic sack. It felt great to be out of them. They were far too big for him, and his feet slid around with no support. Taking his socks off so his feet could breathe, he noticed large blisters already forming. He pulled the wet socks back over his feet and put his own boots back on before giving one last look to the Hastings Salvage Yard.

The smile he wore as he drove off was well beyond batshit crazy.

IX

June 13th, 9:15 A.M:

Thick clouds spread out across the sky like angry gray cotton balls that have been unevenly stretched, blocking out most of the day's light and forcing an eerie gloom on the small town that cast the world in grayscale. Edwin could smell the rain even though it wouldn't start for another few hours. Tall blades of grass had taken over his lawn. It hadn't been mowed since the day before Timothy was taken from him. Maybe he'd put a flyer up in the post office and see if some townie kid wanted to make some cash.

Edwin sat on a plastic lawn chair in his garage, feet propped up on a paint can, looking out through the open bay door. Something he'd seen the old-timers do but had never done himself. He drank a beer from a pilsner glass and watched as a couple of officers came by and removed the police tape from the basement door of the church. All would be hunky-dory Monday morning, and Lincoln could get back to work.

He'd be stupid to go back there. Edwin shook his head and downed the remainder of his beer.

Raising his arms high above his head, he stretched his back as he stood, his spine popped in three places and a relieved moan escaped him. Walking over to the small fridge, he grabbed another can of Coors Light. It gave off a *PSSH* as it cracked open, and he poured it into his glass without allowing any of the foam to rush over the lip. He sat back down in his chair, kicked his feet back up on the paint can, and watched the police toss the trash bag of yellow tape into their cruiser. Officer Martinez wasn't over there, but he hardly expected to see him.

Pastor Simmons talked with the officers briefly. Certainly inviting them to some church function or another, shook their hands, and waved as they drove off. Before turning back to his church, the pastor noticed Edwin and gave him a friendly wave, too. The wave was returned by Edwin lifting his glass in the air.

There really wasn't much distance between Edwin and the pastor, even being on opposite sides of the street, and Edwin could see that the pastor, who was well into his fifties, looked at least a decade older than he had the last time he'd seen the man. The incident at the church must have taken its toll on him. Long afternoons of consoling the families that were there when this tragedy happened definitely showed.

Edwin would have been content not seeing Officer Alex Martinez, who, for a brief time, seemed as if he could have been a good friend. Hell, Edwin hadn't had a true friend in so long that he believed Alex could've become his best friend. Plus, he wasn't even ashamed to be hoping that Lincoln would be a friend after all this had ended.

The basement door banged open across the street, jolting Edwin from his thoughts. He heard it echo through town before echoing in the garage around him. Pastor Simmons glanced around briefly, decided the sound came from somewhere else in the neighborhood, and returned his focus to the other side of the church. Seconds later, Officer Martinez emerged at the top of the steps. From Edwin's angle it appeared that the man emerged from the ground like a zombie rising up from its grave. The officer turned, facing down into the church basement, and made hand gestures as if talking to someone, but whoever it was didn't follow him.

Martinez didn't need to see Edwin sitting in his garage; it was evident in his stride that he was on his way over regardless. A passing car hit the brakes, squealing to a halt, as the officer walked out into the street that separated the church and Edwin's house. The driver brought his hand up to honk, but, realizing it was a cop, decided to keep a low profile while the officer seemed preoccupied.

"Mr. Edwin Fuckin Carmichael," Martinez said. He approached as if he were a man on a mission. There was something ghoulish in the man's voice that shook Edwin from his comfort zone.

"Alex," Edwin said. He hoped to remind the man of their potential friendship and end the officer's tirades.

"A tad early for a beer, isn't it?" It was more than a tad, but before Edwin could reply, Martinez added, "I'll take one if you got an extra."

"Uh, sure. Help yourself." Edwin pointed to the small fridge. From the smell of the man, he really didn't need another drink, but Edwin was already on his bad side and a little afraid of what might happen if Martinez had a complete breakdown.

Martinez pulled up a chair and sat down right next to Edwin. Too close in Edwin's opinion, as he felt the other man's arm hair tangling in his own. Alex cracked the can open and downed it in one pull, then dropped the can on the floor and belched so deeply that Edwin felt it vibrate through him.

The officer was disheveled and looked wore out. Similar to the pastor, Martinez appeared to be much older than the last time Edwin had seen him. His skin had lost some of its elasticity and formed deep wrinkles. Trying not to gag, Edwin tried to ignore the man's smell. It was more than just booze. Perhaps decay.

There was a tinge of sadness and sympathy that Edwin felt for this man, and then Martinez opened his mouth again.

"Well, Fuckface, what're your plans for the day?"

Edwin was shocked by the way this man spoke to him now, but he kept his tempter in check. "What the hell happened to you, man? Just a few days ago you were a good man. You loved God and your family, and you were respectful of everyone. Shit, you put your faith in me during the hardest and most bizarre time in my life."

"Then you betrayed my trust, asshole. I believed that you didn't kill your boy. Then I found his body in that basement. And whatever trap you and that asshole friend of yours set down there went off and killed my partner." Martinez replied in a tone that was all too indifferent.

"I don't know what you saw in that basement, or why you're hanging out over there, but I didn't kill Timothy. I didn't kill Cory, and neither did Lincoln."

Alex made a hand gesture to Edwin saying forget about it and said, "It's all blood under the bridge, man." Edwin had never heard the expression put quite like that but let Martinez continue. "I mean, you're a murderer. We can cut the bullshit now. We're both adults, but for that, I'm going to drop you like a crying baby." Martinez barked with laughter as if he'd just told one hell of a joke.

Edwin stood up and turned away, holding back his anger, counting in his head. He exhaled deeply and said, "I have to get going. I have some things to finish up inside, but it was great talking to you. I hope you get your head sorted out, or maybe looked at by a professional."

"Thanks, I appreciate your concern," Martinez replied in an eerily genuine tone. "You better run on inside. Don't let me keep you. I do have a question though. Do parents who murder their children cry for their loss like those of us who love our children enough to want to see them grow up?"

"Fuck you." Edwin took a step toward the seated man and clenched his fists. "Who the fuck do you think you are? You can't just come over here and talk to me like that." He fought back the urge to swing at the officer and walked into the house through the garage door. He wanted to kill the man, and he knew the only way he wouldn't is to get the hell out of there quickly. Before closing the door he stuck his head out and said, "Why don't you head home and shower? You smell like booze and piss and look like hell. Oh, and go fuck yourself."

Martinez sat in the garage for a few more minutes before standing up and grabbing another beer from the fridge. He finished it in the same manner as the first: one long pull. Tossed the can to the ground and walked out. He could feel Edwin's eyes on him as he crossed the street, as if the man was trying to set him on fire with heat vision. Martinez paid him no attention though, Stevens and the doll were in the basement, and he needed to make sure nothing happened to either of them.

Edwin couldn't believe what just happened, or maybe he could. After what he's experienced, anything's possible. He couldn't help but feel like something much darker than anger and liquor was manning the controls in Martinez' head. The man he'd first met on the night his son was taken had been a caring man with strong family values. He believed in God and the law and was incredibly respectful. Whatever he was now wasn't him, Edwin knew. He wouldn't accept that it was Alex Martinez. It seemed too likely that this demon has found somewhere else to be for the time being instead of harassing him with images of his ex-wife and son. That wasn't any more comforting to think about, however. He continued to stare out the window long after Martinez descended the stairs to the basement.

Clouds continued to gather in the sky. A storm approached. More than likely it wouldn't just be one storm, but a series of storms that would pound down on top of the small town of Kathrine. The sweet, comforting smell of rain closing in thickened. A welcome change as the smell of death had been choking him for a week. He was scared to admit that he could see no way to avoid whatever was about to happen. For now he would just sit back and watch the storm. Ride it out. Hope it passes without doing too much damage.

June 13th, 2:23 P.M:

While Edwin sat on Timothy's bed and watched the graying sky through a window, Officer Alex Martinez had left the church and drove out to Lincoln's house. He parked his police cruiser just at the beginning of the long driveway. He had volunteered to escort Mr. Hoover from Child Protective Services onto the property for their inspection, and ultimately their decision as to whether or not they take Sadie Elizabeth Scott from her parents. Martinez couldn't wait to take that little girl away from her parents. Her pained tears were sweet nectar.

Deep in his deranged thoughts, he hadn't notice he'd been scratching in a perfectly timed duet with a mysterious thumping that his ears couldn't hear but his body knew was there. The yellowing fingernails on his right hand dug deep into the thin flesh over that small bump on his right ankle that a doctor would say is the talus bone. The flesh tore away easily, leaving Martinez to dig into the bone.

"Finally," he said as the black sedan pulled off the main road. It wasn't a day to try his patience. He climbed out of his cruiser and waved. The sedan stopped next to him and the driver's window came down with an electric hum.

"How's it going, Officer?" Mr. Hoover gave a pleasant smile that hid his true question, *what the fuck happened to you? You look like dogshit*.

"Everything's fine," Martinez replied. The white in his eyes was incredibly bright and the retinas appeared more blue than black, but Mr. Hoover assumed it could just be the darkening sky and the officer's color-drained face. "Now, I think for your safety," he paused as if to hold back a cough (or a laugh). "I'll go up to the door first. Then I'll keep the worthless parents away from that little girl, you grab her and burn rubber."

"I'm terribly sorry if there has been any confusion, Officer Martinez, but we are simply checking up on the family. I highly doubt we'll be taking that little girl. It was my understanding that you've been through this before and know how this works. There shouldn't be any problems. The family has already agreed to meet with us today." He eyed the sky and added, "Plus I'd like to make this quick. I want to be home with my own family before the storm hits."

"Oh, yeah, of course. Follow me then." Martinez smiled and held up his bloody right hand as if to say, my bad. Mr. Hoover had just missed it as he rolled up his window, but he soon got a close up view. The right hand, already bloody, crashed through the thick glass with a strength Martinez didn't know he had and grabbed Mr. Hoover's face.

Mr. Hoover tried to scream, but the unnaturally powerful right fist of Officer Martinez struck his throat like a hammer striking the head of a nail. There was a shallow pop as Mr. Hoover's larynx broke. It was hard to breathe, and he quickly became light-headed. He gasped for breath and watched helplessly as Martinez pulled his arm back for another swing. This one was a direct hit to the front of Mr. Hoover's mouth, rattling—chipping, even—his teeth but not knocking any out.

Blood poured down the front of his shirt as he cried out. His lips were busted open and spraying blood like the outlet of a dam. And then it all stopped. Martinez had released him and walked away. There was still a tightening in his throat, what he assumed was swelling from the broken larynx. If he could only make a phone call he might not suffocate. But it was too late. Martinez returned with a freezer bag. It was hard for Mr. Hoover to see through his teary-eyed vision, but it looked as if the officer was carrying a screwdriver that he'd removed from the bag.

Officer Martinez had doubled up on his latex gloves. The screwdriver he carried was six inches long with a black and yellow handle from Lincoln's garage. It was now a missing piece of an entire set. Mr. Hoover's croaks were barely audible anymore. Martinez drove the screwdriver into the man's shoulder, pulled it out, and drove it back into his body. This time it went in just below his left nipple. By the time he was done stabbing, Mr. Hoover had twenty-nine new holes in his body, arranged haphazardly from his lower abdomen to his neck. Small puffs of thought from deep within Alex's mind popped up, begging for him to think about the path he's chosen, but those thoughts were silenced more and more with each stab.

Admiring his handiwork, with a small part of him feeling sick about it, Martinez smiled a deranged smile and looked around to make sure nobody was close by. He pulled the driver's side door open and squeezed in beside the dead Mr. Hoover. With a turn of the key, the car came to life. Alex had done some research when he first arrived at Lincoln's driveway, and that was to confirm the ground was firm.

With the engine firing away and only half of his body in the driver's seat, Martinez put the car in drive and rolled past his cruiser, turned left and rolled off the driveway into the twenty yard strip of yard that sat between the driveway and field that this year was used for beans. Where the field started so did a line of trees that stood between it and the road. Martinez drove along this tree row for what about half a mile before it ended in a cluster of trees and the ruins of an ancient fence.

He parked the car as deep as he could in the cluster with just enough showing to catch his eye as he passed by on the main road later on. Then something clicked in his brain, and that was the fact that he, Martinez, had bled, and that blood was on the body and in the car. He jogged the distance back to his car, popped the trunk, and grabbed a bottle of bleach he'd found in the basement of the church with some other supplies Lincoln had left there.

The jog back to the car was much slower. He was feeling fatigued and wasn't sure if he would be able to even make it back to his cruiser after this, but he finally made it and soaked the crime scene in bleach. Pride swelled in him. A job well done! This isn't exactly what Stevens said they needed to do to catch these fuckers, but there was room in every plan for a little improvisation.

What amazing luck that this shitstain lives so far out in the middle of nowhere that I can set him up in broad daylight. A low, rolling moan rumbled overhead, causing Martinez to look up at the darkening sky. *Well, maybe not broad daylight.* He took the inevitable storm as a good omen. It would keep everyone indoors, buying him enough time to do what he needed to do.

He absentmindedly picked the crud—mostly his own flesh and a little dirt—from his fingernails as he finished the walk back yet again to his awaiting cruiser. Finally making it, he threw the door open and plopped heavily down in the seat, inhaling deeply through his nose and exhaling from his mouth. He couldn't believe how out of shape he'd gotten.

As the first drops of rain splattered on the windshield, Martinez smiled with relief. There was nothing he could do about anything now. This part was out of his hands, come whatever may. Following the plan, his new, revised plan, had consumed him. Putting these murderers behind bars was his goal. He closed the door of the cruiser just as the pitter-patter of rain became a raucous applause.

Applause for a job well done.

June 13th, 2:27 P.M:

"You've been in outer space for a few days, Link. Everything has been great. I think this is all over. This demon thing." Kaydence whispered the last sentence. Not so much because she didn't want Sadie to hear, but because she felt like a lunatic saying it aloud.

"I hope you're right," Lincoln said. His smile was fake but Kaydence wasn't fooled, she understood how he felt right now. At least she thought she did. His shower a few days ago did seem a little long, but she passed it off as a well-earned time of relaxation. It was far from it, and his mood had been fairly somber ever since.

"I'm glad we got the new windows in when we did." He looked out through the new glass at the dark clouds rolling in. "That plastic wouldn't have handled a heavy storm." Lincoln tapped on the glass of a new window. His last two days had been spent installing them with the help of Sadie Elizabeth, who really only smeared the glass and ate animal crackers. It made her happy, however, and that brought Lincoln a little joy, too.

"Where is Sadie?" Kaydence asked. "I figured she'd be down here watching cartoons."

"She must be upstairs." Lincoln continued to stare out the window. "Do you think that Child Services guy is still coming out? He should be here any minute, but I figured he would've called and postponed. Hopefully just cancelled this bullshit altogether."

Kaydence was about to say something, but a soft, distant noise separated itself from the rain and caught her attention. "Do you hear that?"

Lincoln stopped breathing and focused on the sounds. "All I hear is the distant thunder. That's probably all you're hearing also."

"Oh," Kaydence said. She thought briefly of letting it go, but she wasn't convinced. The sound stood out as a consistent thumping. "Things have been pretty strange around here. I think I'll just go up and check on her."

Thump . . . Thump . . . Thump

Fingernails dug into flesh in perfect rhythm with the sound. Flaky skin built up under the long nails like dirt. The loose skin on Lincoln's arm started to break, and it wasn't long before blood trickled down and plopped on the floor in tiny splashes. The pain was only a long lost memory. He stopped and watched out the window. The first drops of rain would be touching down any minute now.

Thump . . . Thump

The sound grew louder as Kaydence climbed the stairs. Only it didn't grow louder to her ears. It grew louder in the space around her. The feeling, something like bass pounding in her chest from a loud stereo, was there, but at the same time, the feeling wasn't physical. It was just a strange presence that fought to be noticed. There was a sound:

Thump . . . Thump

But even as she closed in on it, the audible level remained exactly the same.

"Sadie Elizabeth?" she called out as she pushed the door open. Her eyes widened in horror as she looked in to see her daughter floating in the air. Her arms were apart, chin to her chest, and her feet hung with the right foot in front of the left. "Lincoln!"

When Lincoln heard his wife scream, he stopped scratching, something he still wasn't aware he was doing, and ran up the stairs, taking them two at a time. "What's wrong?" He burst into the room to see Kaydence on her knees in front of their daughter.

"Make it stop!" Tears streaked down Kaydence's face.

Lincoln stepped up to grab ahold of his daughter, but as soon as he touched her a sharp pain shot through him. The little girl's eyes shot open and glared hard at him. He could almost feel the authority in them. They were her eyes, he noticed, and, despite the pain in his body, he found relief in that. But it was short lived.

"In this battle for her soul and the war for all souls," Sadie's voice was sweet, innocent, "*You* will lose."

Thump . . . Thump . . . Thump

Each thump was a pulse that made Sadie's long black hair jump. The invisible shockwave bounced around the room, ruffling the curtains and vibrating the furniture.

"You won't take my daughter!" Lincoln's anger burned the pain away. "Her soul will be mine!" It startled him to hear he'd said that, and he was only sure he had when he saw it had disconcerted Kaydence, as well. She looked at him with shock on her face.

The pulsating thumps continued and a cool wind picked up, whipping around the room. Blankets, coloring books, and stuffed animals were strewn about. One of the curtain rods fell, landing in a heap of pink cloth. Through the window they could see the clouds' persistent darkening. Lincoln's loose skin rippled with each pulse and his knees felt weak.

"Sadie, honey! Can you hear me?" Lincoln yelled.

"Yes, Daddy." She was completely calm.

"You need to fight this demon. Tell me what I need to do to beat this thing." He tried to sound strong but failed.

"You need to die, daddy." Her voice was so innocent.

Kaydence cried harder and massaged her daughter's feet. She was pleading, begging for this to end. "Sadie, please stop this. Make it stop."

The pulsing vibrated Lincoln's bones and his stomach lurched. He ran from the room, slammed the bathroom door open hard enough to crack the bottom when it hit the spring doorstop. Heaving once is all it took for the vomit to roll up and pour from his mouth. His throat was on fire and his eyes watered.

The vomit that splattered in the toilet bowl was bloody with chunks of scabs. Green mucus danced in the mix, giving the overall concoction a festive theme. Lincoln dry heaved several times after that. His body curled as he retched, but nothing else came out. He unrolled a wad of tissue and blew the bloody vomit from his nose, wiped his mouth and chin, and flushed it down. The colors swirled as fresh water rushed in. It took another flush to clear it all down.

Lincoln spit a few times into the sink, washed his hands, and looked in the mirror attached to his new medicine cabinet. His eyes were far more yellow than before and one retina was dilated so wide his entire eye was black. The pulsing stopped, or his body had become numb to its strange sensation. A tuft of hair dropped down into the sink. He reached up and ran his fingers across his scalp, combing out several more good sized clumps.

"What the fuck is happening to me? I must be losing m—" Something jabbed into the roof of his mouth, stopping him mid-sentence. He worked it around and spit a tooth into his hand. He forced a smile into the mirror and looked at the hole where his bottom canine used to sit on the right side. Blood pooled up in its absence. The tooth behind that wiggled as he tongued the bloody opening, so he reached in and was surprised at how easily it came out also.

He tossed both of the teeth into the trash can and spit another mouthful of blood into the sink. Not wanting to see anymore of whatever was happening to his body, he avoided the mirror and walked out of the bathroom. Kaydence could be heard down the hall, crying and begging Sadie to stop. Sadie's little voice telling him he needed to die echoed in his head.

X

June 13th, 5:12 P.M:

Officer Martinez hauled ass to Hastings Salvage in the small town of Gale. The rain and threat of a severe storm had cleared the roads of most drivers for him. With the speedometer's needle climbing over a hundred, his car started to hydroplane, but he maintained control, slowed it down for a quarter mile, and punched the accelerator back down. Things were coming together, and he had to hurry, today would be the day.

But things weren't exactly coming together. A quick stop at the church made him regret the decision to leave Stevens and the doll in the basement. Stevens had told him that the doll should be kept there. It was a safe place for it, but now the doll was gone, and so were Stevens and the pastor. Now wasn't the time to worry about it, though, so he continued on with the rest of his plan.

Yesterday, a Missing Persons Report was filed for one Mr. Brian Hastings. The report, filed by his wife, Sarah, claimed that her husband had come out to check on something late on the night of the eleventh and never came back inside. Rain or shine, Martinez was an officer of the law and planned on getting to the bottom of this.

He'd called earlier and asked for permission to take a look around the salvage yard a little. This had caused poor Mrs. Hastings to panic and sob uncontrollably, something that Martinez quickly tired of hearing. "If you're searching here, that means you think he's dead, doesn't it?" she said in her blubbering sobs. Martinez had told her it was all just protocol in the most comforting voice he could produce.

But Martinez was pretty sure he'd find the body of Mr. Hastings disposed of in the salvage yard. To add to this already baffling disappearance, a ring of his cell about an hour ago led to a conversation with a young woman from Child Protective Services asking Martinez if he'd heard from Mr. Hoover, who also failed to phone into the office regarding his decision on the Scott's and their child. Their notes showed that Mr. Hoover was to meet with Officer Alex Martinez at the Scott residence.

Martinez hadn't heard from the man either, of course, and promptly apologized for being late to the meeting, as he was assisting a stranded motorist in Muscatine a couple miles out from the Scott's home.

The gate to the salvage yard was open as he pulled in. Mrs. Hastings said she'd open it up and he could come and go as he pleased. He cruised back slowly, hoping the wife wasn't around. He couldn't take anymore of her crying. Get over it, sweetheart. *He was worth millions. Find yourself a hot young stud that needs a sugar mamma and buy him a Porsche as payment for filling your needs.*

The cruiser came to a stop; Martinez climbed out onto the wet dirt and walked up and down the row of junked cars before climbing back in and driving up a little further. Stop . . . walk . . . go. He made this his routine for the next hour. He doubted anyone would trace his steps, but he knew how it would look if he lead a search party to the right spot on the first try.

Finally he pulled up next to the old rusty Plymouth Satellite and climbed out into the pouring rain. He looked around at the deserted salvage yard. The place was empty except him and the deceased Brian Hastings. He slid out of his police cruiser and buttoned up his rain jacket. The pouring rain had washed away any visible signs of blood, but after close examination of a few cars, Martinez found clumps of hair and even some flesh on the Satellite.

He walked back to his cruiser and popped the trunk with the button on the key fob, grabbed a crowbar, and returned to the satellite, pried the trunk open again and saw the mess of a man lying inside. Mr. Hastings was caked in a rust-colored blood that complemented the trunk nicely. The smell was really starting to build up, also. Martinez kind of liked it, a provocative aroma.

For a moment, he evaluated the scene, making sure each piece was in place. Climbing back into his cruiser, he called in this gruesome discovery. He would let one of the rookies break the news to that bawling bitch, or he'd end up putting a bullet in her brain. There was no way he could manage such restraint a second time. Before driving off, he pulled up an evidence bag and examined its contents. One sheet of paper would be the nail in the coffin. He'd found the missing clue, and he'd keep it close until the right time. It was a check from Edwin Carmichael to Lincoln Scott for a hundred-thousand dollars.

Alex Martinez felt sick to his stomach. That's all a life cost these days? He tossed the evidence bag down on the passenger's seat and drove off. As the evidence bag hit the seat, the check inside became nothing more than a sales receipt from a hardware store for the purchase of the bricks and mortar.

June 13th, 6:25 P.M:

Edwin sat in his garage, once again thinking of the old-timers sitting in their own garages with their old-timer buddies. Always drinking beer and just enjoying life. He himself was drinking beer but not enjoying life. His son was gone, and he couldn't shake the thought that, if that thing took his soul, they wouldn't even be spending eternity together when this life ended. This ruled out suicide for now, something he found himself considering more and more frequently. He felt that he had to stay alive long enough to defeat this thing and save his son.

The rain beat down on the roof of the garage. The sound resonated around him like a roar. Each heavy drop that hit his Mercedes splashed, giving the car a sparkling diamond look, and for the first time it occurred to him how off that car must look sitting in front of a house that cost less than it did. A heavy stream of the flooding rainwater rushed past the driveway on its way to the bottom of the gently sloped street. Gusts of wind rustled the wet leaves, and thunder rolled high overhead, completing the wonderful orchestra of the storm.

In a distant flash of lightning he saw a figure in the passenger's seat of his car. He studied the now-dark windshield but wasn't able to see anything. Sipping his beer, Edwin held the cold liquid in his mouth for a second. Something about the taste had grabbed hold of his attention and alerted his brain that something wasn't right.

Leaning forward, Edwin spit the mouthful of beer onto the garage floor. The concrete was spattered with blood, and squirming in the blood was maggots. He reached for a roll of blue shop towels, tore a handful from the roll, and wiped his mouth. Peering into the can, he could just make out the wiggling insects. He walked to the open garage door and poured the can out into the driveway and watched the rain wash it away.

The salty taste of blood lingered on his tongue, but he wasn't about to open another can. "You're not going to get in my head," he said. "Whatever you do to me, whatever you show me, you won't scare me."

"Daddy." The word came out sounding more like *naaa-eee*, but someone deep within Edwin it was understood clearly.

Edwin jumped and spun around, facing into the garage. "I told you before, you twisted fuck. Don't use my boy for your games. If you want to come after me do it yourself. I'm nothing to you!" he cried out. "Just end it! Please!"

Timothy stood before his father, sadness in his eyes. Blood seeped uncontrollably from his mouth in thick streams. "Daddy," *naaa-eee*, he said again. This time Edwin could see that his son's tongue was nothing but shredded meat flopping loosely in his mouth. Timothy pointed to Edwin's car.

"What do you want?" He was still convinced this was a trick. Timothy pointed more urgently at the car. Edwin saw something urgent in this terrible image of his son. "Do you want me to go somewhere?"

Timothy nodded, and a bloody tear rolled down his cheek. "Hurry." *Eeer-eee.*

"Where do I need to go?" Edwin asked. He started to cry. He looked at his son. This *was* his son, he had no doubt. In the way that the mother of twins can tell them apart, he knew this *was* his son. Tears streaked down Edwin's face and he dropped to his knees, reaching for his son but unable to touch him. The little boy was a mirage. As Edwin moved toward Timothy, Timothy drifted away.

"I'm so sorry," Edwin sobbed.

Timothy kept pointing at the car.

Edwin nodded his understanding. "I love you, son. I love you so much!"

Timothy's face broke into a smile. It was cruel and grotesque, but Edwin would have given anything to look at the sweet face of his little boy forever. He walked out into the rain and climbed in the car. The smell of blood and rot was thick, but Edwin smiled.

"Let's go for a ride," he said. Although the car was empty, he looked into the rearview mirror and saw Timothy buckled in safely behind him.

June 13th, 6:35 P.M:

Sadie Elizabeth continued to float in the center of her room as if she were being crucified on an invisible cross. Her eyes were closed, her face tranquil. She appeared to be asleep, which made Kaydence wonder if that was the cause of the phantom thrumming slowing down. She stood beside her daughter with her arms wrapped around the little girl's waist in a protective embrace. She tried to pull her down, but Sadie clung firmly to the air she was suspended from.

The rain pounded against the side of the house while the wind whistled against the siding. The roar of the rain has always been something Lincoln found comforting, not this afternoon. This was a bad day to be caught in a storm. A severe weather alert flashed across Lincoln's cellphone, sounding out in that all too familiar blare heard on the TV or radio, but he was too preoccupied to pay any attention to it. After calling Pastor Simmons, he tossed the phone down and paced back and forth by the front door.

Headlights lit up the yard as a car trudged down the long, flooded driveway. Pastor Simmons told Lincoln it would be about twenty minutes before he could get there. It had taken him ten. The station wagon pulled up close to the house. Simmons swung the car door open, climbed out carefully, and made his way up to the covered porch quickly. He held a briefcase over his head to shield himself from the pounding rain and occasional pellets of hail.

"Thank you for coming, Pastor," Lincoln said. He stood waiting on the porch.

"I don't know how much help this old body can be, Lincoln, but I wouldn't turn my back on you." The pastor offered his hand to Lincoln. Lincoln shook it, cupping it between both his hands.

As Lincoln started to close the door he saw a new set of lights bouncing down the driveway. "What the hell?" he asked before apologizing to the pastor who waved it off with a smile. He stepped back out onto the porch where the rain beating on the roof thundered in his ears.

The car came to a stop behind the pastor's station wagon. Lincoln could see the three-pointed star of the Mercedes-Benz logo glistening in the porch light. Edwin stepped out and jogged carefully through the rain. He gave both Lincoln and the pastor a wave, but Lincoln could see the untrusting look Edwin shot at Pastor Simmons as he stepped into the light.

"What are you doing out here?" Lincoln asked. "It probably isn't safe to be on the road." He urged the men into the shelter of his house.

Edwin shook the water from his jacket before walking inside. He closed the door behind him and kept his eyes on the pastor. "Timothy told me I needed to come here."

Lincoln trusted the man enough to take him on his word, and he was thankful to have him here. However, he did sense a growing tension between Edwin and Pastor Simmons. The pastor, who had been pleasant when he arrived, now appeared a bit unsettled.

"Where is Sadie?" Pastor Simmons asked, turning his attention away from Edwin and showing concern for the little girl.

"Follow me," Lincoln said. As he started leading the two men upstairs he was interrupted by Pastor Simmons.

"I mean no offense, Lincoln, but I believe your friend should wait down here. Too many people being up there can create a lot of risks for your daughter." Pastor Simmons showed even more concern. "This *despicable* demon may draw strength from everyone around it."

"I can wait here," Edwin said before Lincoln had to waste any time considering what the pastor had said.

Lincoln nodded and led the pastor to Sadie's bedroom.

The door was open, and both men could see Kaydence curled up on the floor under Sadie's feet. Panic set in and he ran in hoping that his wife was alright. He brushed the hair from her face and she opened her eyes. At first she smiled at him, but she realized that the events she'd been dealing with were real.

"Oh God, Lincoln." She saw the pastor standing in the doorway and felt uncomfortable with her choice of words. "Is everything going to be alright? Can he stop this?"

"I don't know if I can or not, Mrs. Scott. I'm going to do everything I can to make sure this night goes as planned," Pastor Simmons said.

Kaydence found she wasn't comforted by the pastor. His choice of words cycled through her mind as she tried to pick out what he'd meant by them. She was bothered more and more by the man, and she was just about to speak up when Sadie's eyes opened and the thumping returned in full force.

"You're on the wrong side of this, Pastor," Sadie said in a powerful, deep voice. The room trembled as she spoke.

"If Sadie is in there, you need to fight this demon inside you," the pastor said. He turned to Lincoln and Kaydence. "I've never done this before, so stick with me, please."

"Of course. We'll do whatever you need." Lincoln looked to Kaydence to see that she understood.

Kaydence had dropped her concerns for the pastor momentarily, as a much more pressing matter was at hand.

"Good. You'll have to do exactly what I say without question . . . and without hesitation," Pastor Simmons urged. "I assure you that no harm will come to little Sadie. This creature doesn't have the strength to compete with the power of—" His eyes opened wide as the word hung in his throat.

"Are you alright, pastor." Lincoln ran over to help the man.

A long vein bulged in Pastor Simmons' forehead, and he crammed his index finger deep into his mouth. He gagged and heaved as he pulled out a large clump of black hair. The mass of hair was enough to fill his entire mouth and hit the floor with a wet splat. It looked like something pulled from a clogged shower drain.

"You will leave this girl's body," the pastor croaked as he gasped for breath. "You have no place on this earth. Not anymore."

The wind rattled the windows and dime-sized pellets of hail came down with the rain, pelting the glass and siding. The sound was that of a thousand little hands knocking, begging for admittance, wanting nothing more than shelter from the storm. The floor creaked as the pulsating thrum worked its way through the house.

Pastor Simmons picked his briefcase up and laid it down on the dresser. He flicked the brass clasps out of their locked position and opened the case, revealing several glass vials and the doll, Bethesda. Seeing the doll again made Lincoln nervous, but right now he had to put his trust in the pastor. Any doubts he may have had were pushed aside.

As the pastor lifted Bethesda from the briefcase, Sadie let out a low hiss that sounded like a car tire deflating after running over a nail. There was no anger or fear in the sound, just loathing. The room vibrated hard enough for Lincoln to feel it moving underneath him.

"This won't hurt you, Sadie. It's going to remove this beast that has taken up host inside your body." Pastor Simmons stepped closer to her. Sadie's body tensed and her breathing—the pulsing, as well—sped up as he did so. "You need to relax," he said as he held the doll in front of him like a shield.

The entire room lit up with flashes of red and blue. Neither Lincoln nor Kaydence had any idea of what demonic illusion it could be until Edwin yelled from the bottom of the stairs. His voice was faint over the wind, rain, and pulsating thump, but what he said came through clear enough to cause Lincoln's heart to race faster than it already was.

"The cops are here!" Edwin shouted. He wasn't sure if Lincoln had called them, but the last time he checked, protect and serve didn't cover demonic possessions. He watched through the window as four police cruisers cut through the grass of Lincoln's front lawn, braking hard and leaving long ruts in the sopping dirt. *Lincoln's going to be pissed about that*, he thought and shook his head.

Edwin walked to the door and reached to open it just as a deep voice on a bullhorn bellowed over the roar of the storm. The booming voice startled him, and he stepped back into the dark kitchen. The whole interior of the house flashed blue and red with the occasional glimpse of purple as the two primary colors mingled.

"Lincoln Scott!" the voice erupted. "This is Sergeant Sean Williams of the Muscatine County Police Department. We are asking that you and Mr. Edwin Carmichael come outside. Nobody has to be hurt. Come out with both hands raised above your heads."

"Oh shit," Edwin whispered.

Upstairs, Lincoln listened to the loud voice in confusion. *What the hell do they want?* "You stay here with Pastor Simmons and Sadie. I'll be right back."

"Is everything going to be alright?" Kaydence asked as his hand slipped away from hers.

"Yeah, I'm sure there's just a misunderstanding," he said and gave her a warm smile.

Standing in the pouring rain, Officer Martinez started his walk through the sopping wet grass. He aimed his flashlight into Lincoln's truck and nodded to another officer. "His boots are here! Looks like there's dirt and maybe some blood." He opened the door and reached in with a gloved hand, picked up one of the boots and turned it over in the light. "Definitely blood," he confirmed.

Another officer came over and carefully placed the boots into an evidence bag. None of the other officers thought to question how Martinez seemed to be lucky enough to make these discoveries. Hell, on the way in he managed to spot a distant glimmer of chrome in a lightning flash that turned out to be the car that belonged to Mr. Hoover. The unfortunate Mr. Hoover was still in it, stabbed to death with a screwdriver that was left on the floor. Officer Martinez had police work in his blood, and tonight it was pumping like jet fuel through a dragster. Tonight . . . he was on it.

Until he walked up onto the porch of Lincolns house and opened the door.

"Officer Martinez," a distant voice yelled. "You need to step away from the hou—"

Two officers ran up to cover him until they could clear the area, and as the three officers stepped through the front door, it banged shut behind them. One of the officers, an older man with a thick blond mustache, attempted to open the door with no luck, while a young officer kept his sidearm drawn to the situation inside. The younger man's heart raced as he looked into the dimly lit family room.

"Hello," Martinez called. He smiled wide and looked as if he were having one hell of a good time. "Yoo-hoo." Turning toward the kitchen, he spotted Edwin standing in the dark. "A-ah, there's one of you. Where's your buddy at? You can tell me. We're old friends me and you."

"You look like ass, Alex. Look at yourself, man. You're sick or something," Edwin said. Despite feeling scared out of his mind, he managed to slow his heart rate down to normal. He was cool and collected.

Martinez smiled and let out of deranged chuckle. Edwin could see that he was missing several teeth. The officer raised both arms up quickly and flexed, wrinkled skin hung loosely. "This is a hundred-and-sixty pounds of twisted steel and sex appeal, my friend. I'm in the best shape of my life, and I feel pretty fucking amazing."

Now both officers behind Martinez had their guns drawn, facing Edwin.

"What's the problem, officers?" Lincoln asked as he appeared at the top of the stairs. Both of his hands were raised above his head. Edwin noticed that Lincoln also looked to be aging rapidly and checked his own skin. He was relieved to see it was still taut over his body.

"You are both under arrest for the murders of Mr. Brian Hastings, Mr. Mark Hoover, Timothy Carmichael, and most importantly . . . Officer Cory Stevens." Martinez looked back and forth between the two men. His eyes were brilliantly bright (unnaturally (supernaturally)), consuming everything they saw, obsessing over every little detail, and waiting for someone to make their move.

"That's fucking crazy, and you know it," Lincoln said as he took a step down the stairs. "Neither of us killed anybody." He took another step. His knees ached as he did. Deep in the space around him, Lincoln could feel something dark. The light radiating from the fixtures seemed to be pulled from the air.

"And neither of you are going to be arrested for it, either," Martinez said. He was composed and spoke matter-of-factly.

"What do you mean?" Edwin asked. He shuffled slowly into the family room just below the staircase, arms also raised, and met Lincoln at the bottom. The men stood just several feet apart and faced Martinez.

"I mean you're both going to die tonight." Martinez unholstered his Beretta.

At first, Edwin thought the flash he saw was lightning, cracking the dark sky outside. It wasn't until the stream of blood running down his shirt told him that he was mistaken. There was very little pain. His body was in shock, and his mind failed, or refused to register that a small lead slug tore through his heart.

He was caught by Lincoln, who screamed at the officers standing before them. Screams from the two officers that came in with Martinez intertwined with Lincoln's to create a stereophonic effect, but the sounds were so far away that Edwin had to strain to hear if there were any real words buried within the noise. Before he closed his eyes forever, he looked into the face of Martinez, who appeared to be in more physical pain than he was. His final thought was of his son.

"You motherfuckers!" Lincoln shouted, looking up at the trio of cops in his living room. Warm blood poured from Edwin's chest and mouth and ran across the floor. "What the hell is wrong with you?"

The pain slowly faded from Martinez' face, as if he had also died. It was replaced with a look that made Lincoln think of someone hating and loving something simultaneously. Then he smiled and raised his Beretta, aiming execution style at Lincoln's head.

"It's all part of His plan," Martinez said. "You have to die." Ignoring the officers behind him, Martinez pulled the trigger and the second muzzle flash lit the room. The gunshot rang through the air, but the bullet slid out of the barrel and hit the floor with a soft clang.

The black figure stood in front of Lincoln protectively. At first it appeared to be nothing more than rolling smoke from the gunshot, but within seconds it thickened into a solid form. A black cloth dropped from the figure's back like a cloak, only than it split down the middle with a sickening tear and pulled apart. Fine black feathers materialized in the massive wings that stretched from the shoulder blades to the floor before flapping out to display an impressive wingspan that would have easily reached twenty feet if it weren't for the confines of the room.

Lincoln felt the pain in his joints and his skin burned slightly as the massive black angel standing before him pulled energy from his body. His skin cracked as it dried before his eyes and his teeth ached. Martinez stared at the figure menacingly, and blood trickled from his nose.

"You will not interfere here. You can't be everywhere at once," the black angelic figure stated. Its voice was wet, cold and menacing.

The two officers behind Martinez began to scream in pain. The older man placed his hands over his bulging eyes, but it wasn't enough to keep them from bursting. Thick white liquid oozed down his cheeks. Terrible crunching sounds escaped his head as the air pressure around him caused his skull to collapse, pushing his brains out through his ears and nose.

The younger officer slowly began leaning backward until his head touched the floor. His feet remained firmly planted on the ground. Continuing to bend, the man's stomach burst open, spraying his guts upward like a geyser. Both officers dropped to the floor next to each other.

Martinez winced as whatever psychic energy assailed him and his companions, but the forces protecting him were strong enough to protect him until his mission was complete.

XI

Edwin opened his eyes and gasped for breath. However deeply he inhaled, what little oxygen he pulled in just wasn't enough to soothe his burning lungs. His chest felt heavy, as well. A great weight bore down on him, but there was nothing but open air above him. The world around him was bland. The dry, brown earth beneath him gave way to the pale-blue sky. The colors where muted and looked as if the landscape around him had been painted with gouache; some spots were thicker, heavier, while other spots seemed worn and thin.

The only sound aside from Edwin's panicked rustling was a thump that echoed from far away.

Then the dry ground behind him crunched with soft footsteps.

"Hello, Edwin."

Edwin sat up and looked into the bearded face of a man in robes that were once black but were now dusty and sun-faded. He had the sad eyes of a man who'd lost everything, but he smiled at the man lying in the dirt. His hand extended from his robe, and Edwin took it without thought, as if something in the man's face told him it would be ok.

"It's hard to breathe," Edwin complained. He looked up at the man pleadingly, hoping there was some way for this stranger to help him.

"Then stop trying," the man responded.

Edwin was sure that was one of the dumbest things he'd ever been told to do, but decided it must have been a joke. Gasping first for any oxygen he could pull from the air around him he said, "Who are you, and where are we?"

"My name is Judas Iscariot. You are in a land far from your own. And I assure you, my friend, if you stop breathing, it will be much better."

"You're Judas? *THE* Judas?"

Judas found this man to be strangely peculiar, but nodded his head. "You must follow me. There isn't much time."

"Where are we going?" Edwin asked. For a moment he'd forgotten to breathe, making his head clear and the pain subside, but his thoughts soon returned to the lack of breathing, and he found himself in pain once more.

Judas started walking, ghostly wisps of dust puffed up under his sandaled feet with each crunching step. "I am taking you someplace special."

"Oh God! I'm dead?" Edwin asked but knew the answer. The realization setting in caused his heart to race and his breathing increased. Only his heart wasn't beating at all. Edwin's head hurt as he gasped for any amount of oxygen his lungs could get.

"You *are* dead, my friend. That is why you *need* to stop breathing. It is only causing you agony. You are feeling no true pain, just the lost remnants of it. There is a yearning to feel it again."

Edwin force himself to stop breathing and the pain subsided. The more the pain ceased, the more he realized that he didn't even have the urge to breathe. It was no longer an automatic function controlled by his brain. It had just stopped, and he felt like it was natural. "Is this Heaven?" He really hoped not.

"No," Judas said. "You are in a world between your own and ours."

"Purgatory?"

"You can call it that if you wish." Judas kept walking as if he were an impatient tour guide.

"So what is my fate?"

Judas didn't answer.

"What about my son? Some demon stole my son." The words felt strange coming out. He wasn't sure if Judas would believe him or not but remembered what Lincoln had told him . . . while he was still alive.

"Not a demon. A Fallen Angel."

"What do you mean?"

"You ask many questions, my friend, but we have some time, so I'll answer this one. Many years ago, there was a war in Heaven. An angel called Lucifer, a truly magnificent and beautiful angel, decided that he was no longer content with his station. He corrupted the minds of several other angels and formed a small legion. As you probably know, that legion failed in their assault, and Lucifer was cast out of Heaven."

"So Lucifer, Satan, *THE* Devil has stolen my son and is possessing Lincoln's daughter?" Edwin interrupted.

Judas shook his head slowly. "Lucifer is far too great. No mortal would survive even a moment in his presence before their body was shattered. I understand your impatience, my friend, but I'll get there."

Edwin only nodded his apology.

"In our time, Jesus Christ and I set out to free a young girl called Adina from the possession of what was believed to be a demonic entity. We failed to do so, and her soul had melded with that of this creature. Jesus came to believe that he had to die in order to find the answers to freeing her soul. I had to betray my best friend, my brother, to ensure his death. His life was worth fortunes far greater than the earthly world could supply, and his death would be worth more still. I allowed our friends, Jesus' family, to believe that I betrayed him out of greed and jealousy." Judas shrugged it off as if he didn't care. As long as people believed in Jesus, that is all he cared about.

"In his death, Jesus sought his answers, and he battled Bethesda–the entity the girl and this creature had become–for Adina's soul. God's power fueled Jesus, but he knew that the girl's soul would be lost forever if he defeated Bethesda there. It wasn't until just several decades ago in your time that we discovered the entity possessing Adina was not a demon, but instead an angel called Xamreyel. One of God's closest and most trusted confidantes.

"Xamreyel had been corrupted by Lucifer long before the war but was clever enough to go undetected in the Lord's ranks. He set out with a mission to destroy Jesus. And this accidental merging of the angel and Adina's soul created a new being far more powerful than any angel, and lacked many of the weaknesses that plague the demons."

Edwin opened his mouth and asked a question before

his mind had totally settled on doing so, "But Jesus' death made him a hero. Wouldn't destroying him have had the same effect? He would have died for our sins, right?"

"Not quite, Jesus' life and teachings would have been celebrated all the same, but his death had to have a stronger meaning to truly carry his words for eternity. But it wasn't just Jesus' *life* that was in danger. His *soul* was, as well. Jesus has protected this world ever since his death. Xamreyel needs him out of the way so Lucifer can spread his evil. Although God's power is eternal and great, he has been at his weakest since he stopped investing himself in the lives of man. By allowing man to follow his own path, man's natural curiosity and emotions have led them in all directions. Corruption and sin, lack of faith throughout the world, has given evil entities such as Xamreyel—Bethesda—tremendous power in this world."

"So what does Timothy have to do with this? Sadie? Are they just collateral damage? Did my boy die for nothing? Will I ever see him again?" Edwin inhaled deeply out of habit, spurring a round of gasps that made him think he was suffocating until he remembered he doesn't need to breathe.

"You son's death was just the beginning. There are sacrifices that have to be made during war. I've made some terrible calls—"

"My son is just a *sacrifice*? For a war he has no part in?" Edwin could feel the anger boiling inside him.

"We all have a part in this war, Edwin. It isn't just the heavens that are threatened." Judas came to a stop and ignored the rest of Edwin's angered rant.

When Edwin finally stopped shouting and realized they'd stopped moving, he looked in the direction Judas was facing. His jaw dropped as he beheld the sight before him. With the pale-blue sky for a backdrop, and the sun-scorched brown earth of this accursed land that he was in, he looked at a lone cross standing at the top of the hill. Walking toward him from that cross was a man he'd recognize just as easily as Santa Claus or Ronald McDonald.

"Jesus Christ," Edwin gasped.

June 13th, 7:08 P.M:

Edwin's limp body hit the ground with an unforgiving thud. The sound itself was like a shock of a long fall felt in the bones, making Lincoln wince, but he couldn't help but drop his now dead friend. Martinez had charged directly at him. The black angel that stood up to protect him was now preoccupied with the bloody mess that was Officer Stevens. Lincoln's mind couldn't catch up with everything he was seeing through the foggy haze of his watery eyes. Stevens had emerged from the mangled pile of flesh and guts that used to be the two unfortunate officers that followed Martinez inside before the door shut and sealed itself, becoming an impenetrable barrier.

Martinez speared Lincoln, slamming his shoulder into Lincoln's stomach hard enough to knock the wind out of him and wrapped his aged, wrinkled fingers around Lincoln's neck. "Your demon can't save you!" Martinez screamed. Droplets of spit and blood peppered Lincoln's face. "It is His will. You have to die. You've been chosen, Lincoln, but you've been chosen to die, so just . . . fucking . . . die!"

Lincoln felt the grip around his neck tighten, and he found he really had to work to pull in oxygen. A vein in the side of his head throbbed visibly like a pulsating root in some eighties horror flick. His mind stumbled on what Martinez said. My demon? What was that supposed to mean? His body was too weak to fight, and if that was his demon, it better get its ass in gear and help.

As if in answer to his thoughts a deep drone ululated through the air like a melancholy fog horn being blasted in his face. The sound wasn't loud, but it was certainly felt, and the walls creaked and splintered as they contracted inward several inches as if by too much pressure on the exterior of the house. Lincoln's blurry vision cleared for that one moment and he saw the black angel and Officer Stevens in a battle that looked too primitive for spirits.

They wrestled, arms intertwined, grappling, battling to be the first to turn the other and drive their opponent to the floor. There was no doubt that the black angel was Bethesda, but why would it be fighting with Stevens, a spirit that Lincoln was positive Bethesda sent here to corrupt Stevens.

Stevens countered the opposing pull and flung himself inwards, getting his arms wrapped around Bethesda's blackened frame; its wings brushed wildly, one tip scraping the wall between the front door and kitchen while the other scratched the screen of the TV on the other side of the room before sending it crashing to the floor, both entities cried out. Bethesda's cries were deep and sinister while the sound from Stevens was calm and angelic. An angel and a demon fought before Lincoln, and he couldn't decide which was which.

Bethesda worked one arm free, reached into the large hole in Stevens' body, gripped the dead man's spine, and pulled out several of the vertebrae. Stevens became unstable, his body leaning backward slightly, but continued to fight. Soft bursts of blackness exploded from the dead officer's eyes, sucking the light out of the air around them for several feet. Each one of these dark flashes caused long black feathers to drop from Bethesda's wings and strips of the creatures dry flesh peeled away.

Sensing a brief opening, Stevens picked Bethesda up and slammed the being into the floor hard enough to turn the wood flooring into a spider web of cracks. Welding an obviously unnatural force, Stevens continued to push until the two entities broke through the floor and disappeared out of site.

Only a moment of calm followed before the two shot up through the hole. Bethesda held Stevens' head in one hand and slammed the dead officer up into the ceiling. Chunks of plaster and dust fell to the floor. Bethesda's mouth opened wide to reveal teeth as black as the charcoaled flesh that wrapped the being's body.

The droning blare echoed again, sending a bolt of pain tearing through Martinez' body and knocked more chunks of the ceiling loose. His grip slackened and oxygen flooded Lincoln's lungs. He was still weak but managed to roll the deranged officer off him. Looking around the room, he noticed that Stevens had also momentarily halted his attack on Bethesda.

What the fuck is going on? he thought.

Kaydence's scream from upstairs pushed the bizarre scene he was witnessing from his mind and a newfound strength surged through him. Lincoln climbed to his feet and bolted for the stairs.

"Kaydence!" he yelled. Skipping the last few stairs he rounded the landing and pushed forward with as much strength as his legs could provide. He slammed into the closed door of Sadie's bedroom, driving his shoulder into it like a battering ram. The crack that Kaydence had put in it the other day was splintering outward, and Lincoln shifted his attention from trying to bust the door open to busting through it.

"Stay away from her!" Kaydence's voice ripped through the door.

They must be fighting the demon. Then what the fuck *is happening downstairs?* Lincoln thought, continuing to throw his frail body into the door. It cracked and groaned against his weight, finally surrendering to his efforts. Thin chunks of the plywood and stamped hardboard innards fell to the floor as he worked his way through the opening.

On the floor in the center of the room was Sadie. Her eyes were open, but she looked as if she'd frozen in place. Pastor Simmons and Kaydence were wrestling on the floor beside the little girl. A quick shimmer of a blade glinting in the dim light caught Lincoln's eye, and he realized his wife was trying to pull the knife away from the pastor.

"He's trying to kill her!" she cried out.

Lincoln wasted no time. He jumped on top of the pastor and began prying the knife from his fingers.

"Stop, Lincoln," he begged. "You know we have to do this. We have to set our master free. In order to do that, your daughter has to die. You were chosen, Lincoln. You were chosen to help rule, to be a king!"

Lincoln flashed back to the voice he'd heard, speaking soothingly, terrifyingly, in his head. The terrible, dark voice that told him he was chosen for this. Bethesda had spoken to him, came to him, promised it all to him. Bethesda loved him. But the pastor couldn't know that. Lincoln no longer knew whose side he was on.

"I won't let you hurt my little girl," Lincoln said. An explosion of images popped off rapidly like a string of fireworks. There was an inner struggle that threatened to tear him asunder. He watched his daughter's life leave her eyes and his gut wrenched. He wanted to die. He saw Kaydence ripped apart by the demon downstairs, her intestines strung out like streamers as she begged for death.

And in the midst of it, he stood before the woman he'd been with in the shower as she caressed him with her soft, wrinkled fingertips, and they were joined by Kaydence. The pleasure overcame the pain and fear. The three of them made love in a large, soft bed in a room where they walls and floor were made of metals and rocks so rare they couldn't be found anywhere but that room. Their ecstasy was deep and eternal. He and Kaydence sat on thrones with cushions wrapped in the most exotic of furs, wore the finest of silks, and were fed the most flavorful fruits that would never be grown on Earth.

He looked back into Sadie's lifeless eyes and tore painfully away from the visions. He grabbed his wife and pulled her from Simmons.

"What the hell are you doing, Lincoln." She clawed at his gray, wrinkled arms and tried to swing her fist backward at him, but he held her firmly.

"I'm so sorry, babe." Lincoln stroked her hair softly with his free hand. "If she dies, we get everything."

"NO!" she screamed. Driving her heel down into his foot had no effect. She bent her knees slightly and propelled herself off the floor. Lincoln held firm, but she managed to throw him off balance. As she came down, she slipped through his arms just a few inches and launched herself upward once again. This time, the back of her head collided with Lincoln's face.

Blood sprayed from his nose and trickled from his smashed upper lip. Several teeth hit the floor with a soft knock. He cried out more in anger than in pain and threw her to the floor. "You bitch!" he screamed.

She looked up from the floor at him. Tears streaked down her face. She was stunned by this grisly transformation. In the matter of seconds he had gone from trying to protect Sadie to letting the pastor try and kill her. She was appalled by both of them and wasn't even surprised to see that Lincoln was taking on an outer appearance that suited his actions.

The man she loved—she still loved him, he was in there somewhere—was wrinkled and pale. He looked much older than Pastor Simmons, as if something had taken its toll on his body. A fly landed on his face and scurried in a jagged line up his cheek where it settled in at the inner corner of his eye. Then she realized what was happening. The demon hadn't possessed their little girl, it had possessed Lincoln.

Then what has been possessing Sadie?

Lincoln's yellowing eyes opened wide in excitement as he watched the pastor raise the knife high and bring it down toward Sadie. He would be a king, and Kaydence would come to forgive him in time. The knife pierced soft flesh. Fear and pain and sadness surged, but only for a second. The heart was sliced cleanly in two. Blood pumped out in wild spurts.

Sadie screamed, but only for a second.

"Jesus Christ," Edwin said. He struggled with the phrase. He had spoken the name many times in surprise or anger, but now he spoke it in recognition.

Jesus walked down the slope of this uncanny interpretation of Calvary Hill, a landmark Edwin wouldn't have recognized. His eyes sparkled magnificently as he smiled at Edwin. In tatters, his dusty linen robe fluttered around his ankles with each step. His dark brown hair, knotted and tangled, hung down past his shoulders and gave way to the shaggy beard that wrapped around his face.

"There isn't much time, Edwin. We can save your son. We can save them all." Jesus' voice was calm and almost hypnotic in its kindness.

"How?" Edwin asked. He was eager to help, if mostly to save his son.

Jesus motioned for Edwin to follow, and the three of

them walked past the large cross protruding from the dry, cracked earth. The wood was worn and splintered with deep ravines carved out by trickling streams of blood. The sight of this powerful object gave him goosebumps and filled him with an unwavering love and respect for the humble man he now followed. Jesus knew this would be his death, and he welcomed it and the pain it would bring him to save humanity's soul.

No sooner than he'd turned to look away from the large cross it was gone. Left far behind as they moved at a pace that felt to Edwin as if they were leisurely strolling along but must have been moving at an amazing speed he couldn't comprehend. All at once, as if someone had changed the channel, the dry earth below them was a vast ocean with no end in sight.

Edwin felt his heart race, or at least he wanted to. One last time is all he asked.

"Xamreyel believes that by defeating me, he can free the world from its faith in God," Jesus started. "But the fallen angel is blinded by corruption. By possessing Lincoln, Xamreyel has drawn me to his daughter. I must admit that I fell for his tricks. I did what I felt was right to protect her, the way I couldn't protect Adina. But now a part of my essence is with the child, and by killing her, I can be trapped."

Edwin listened. He was amazed by the way the words Jesus spoke were the same simple words everyone else use, but the power in those words made everything else seem insignificant. Edwin thought that maybe only writers could believe that words alone could have such authority.

"So Bethesda possessed *both* Lincoln and Martinez?"

"No. Bethesda has possessed Lincoln only and corrupted the mind of Pastor Simmons." Judas' voice caused Edwin to start. Judas had been so quiet walking beside his companion that Edwin all but forgot he was still with them.

"Well, what about Martinez? He was a great man, and now he's come completely unhinged." Edwin stated.

Judas looked at Jesus, who returned the look with a nod that said it's all you.

Judas continued, "We believe that all people should have free will. So instead of taking control of Martinez . . . I *steered* him in the direction of *our* goals. I spoke with him and gave him a message. Unfortunately, when people are angry and filled with hate, messages become skewed. Jesus and I see it every time we look upon your world. Alex Martinez has proven to be far more chaotic than either of us imagined, but those he's hurt will be rewarded greatly for their sacrifice."

Martinez' voice echoed in Edwin's brain. *You are both under arrest for the murders of Mr. Brian Hastings, Mr. Mark Hoover, Timothy Carmichael, and most importantly . . . Officer Cory Stevens.*

"Oh God!" Edwin gasped than covered his mouth with both hands hoping he didn't just offend either of these men. "He's killed people!" The shock in his voice almost came out as a whine. "He's killed people to frame Lincoln and myself. But why?"

"Our plan was to separate Lincoln from Sadie, to protect her. In order for Xamreyel to complete his transition and become a powerful entity in the world, Lincoln has to sacrifice his own flesh and blood to the fallen angel." Judas stated. "The mother can also sacrifice the girl, but Xamreyel would not gain as much power from her. It would still be enough, but not as much."

"I know I haven't known Lincoln for long, but I would bet my life," Edwin thought about his situation for a second. "I'd bet my *soul* that that man would never harm his little girl."

"Luckily for Xamreyel, Lincoln doesn't have to be in control of his body for her to be made a proper sacrifice. Xamreyel can take over as long as the girl's life is taken by her father." Judas replied.

"Which is why I have been trying to protect her. If I could—" Jesus started but was interrupted.

"Why didn't you try to protect *my* son?" Edwin asked. All at once his anger was searing through his flesh. "Timothy wasn't good enough for you to protect?"

"I would give my soul to protect your son, Edwin. But Xamreyel—Bethesda—was released so quickly that we couldn't act soon enough." There was deep pain in Jesus' eyes that made Edwin feel unworthy of his kindness and a little ashamed he snapped at him.

"What do we need to do to stop this thing forever?" Edwin asked. "Is there a way to save Adina? My son?"

"We have faith that there is," Judas said. "I assure you that you will be reunited with Timothy. We were not expecting to deal with Xamreyel again so soon. From what we have learned, the fallen angel cannot be stopped until Jesus returns to earth. The guardians of the Order of Onyx and Light were supposed to keep Bethesda safe until then."

"Are you talking about the Second Coming of Christ?" Edwin felt astonishment wash over him. Learning that everything he has chosen to ignore is true was a hard pill to swallow.

Before he got an answer, muffled red and blue flashes illuminated the sky. Wet grass squished beneath Edwin's shoes and he looked at Lincoln's house from the outside. Police officers banged frantically on the door to no avail. Windows deflected fists, gun butts, and batons as the officers struggled to get inside to stop the pandemonium.

Xamreyel's power was too great, but it didn't stop Edwin and his new friends from walking past and into the home.

Edwin moaned as he saw his body lying on the floor but felt relief that Lincoln's body wasn't beside him. The distorted screams rolled in slow-motion down the steps, and they followed them to Sadie's bedroom where the door was closed but the middle had been busted down. He stepped through and noticed that Jesus and Judas held their places in the hallway.

Inside the room, Sadie lay motionless on the floor. Lincoln stood beside the pastor with blood gushing from his face. Kaydence sat in the corner, her mouth was contorted in a terrified scream as she tried to scramble to her feet in time to save her daughter. Pastor Simmons brought a long knife down toward Sadie's chest. The scene was like staring into a 3-D image created by a madman.

But beside him was the horrific vision of Officer

Stevens, his guts drying on the front of his uniform. There was a calm smile that said everything would be alright. And Edwin believed it. Emerging from Stevens was the deranged looking form of Martinez. It caused Edwin to double-take as the officer stepped out of Stevens like he'd just walked through a doorway. Then Stevens told Edwin—Not through words or vision, but through the psychic link that old friends seem to have between one another—that he just had to follow his lead and together they could stop this.

And Jesus spoke, "As enough of my essence is attached to Sadie to trap me with her death, enough of Xamreyel's is attached to Lincoln."

XII

June 13th, 7:13 P.M:

Lincoln's yellowing eyes opened wide in excitement as he watched the pastor raise the knife high and bring it down toward Sadie. He would be a king, and Kaydence would come to forgive him in time. The knife pierced soft flesh. Fear and pain and sadness surged, but only for a second. The heart was sliced cleanly in two. Blood pumped out in wild spurts.

Sadie screamed, but only for a second.

Lincoln stared into the confused face of Pastor Simmons. There was a curious betrayal in the pastor's eyes that said he didn't want to believe what had just happened. Blood poured out onto his hands as he continued to hold the knife handle. The blade, all nine inches of it, was buried in Lincoln's chest.

Standing behind the pastor was Officer Martinez. He had once looked disturbed and sick, but he now stood confident and in some way whole. Martinez had grabbed the pastor, spinning him aside with such great force at the last second. He wasn't there a minute ago, *where did he come from*, Lincoln wondered.

With his mouth hanging open and the world around him fading, Lincoln searched the room for his wife and daughter. He wished to see them one last time. Hopefully they'd forgive him, but he knew he didn't deserve it. He was surprised to see that, standing next to Martinez was Stevens. Behind him was Edwin. And it all clicked in his brain.

He had attempted to murder his child. He had been possessed, and Martinez, with the help of Edwin, had stopped it. But he didn't want to focus on the details, details that seem so minor all of a sudden. He knew his life was ending fast. A smile spread across his bloody face as he saw Sadie Elizabeth, crouching on her bed, tears rolling down her cheeks. Her pain tore him up inside, but she was still alive, and that brought him at least a little peace.

His wife was only a blur before his eyes closed forever.

Kaydence had witnessed Martinez appear in the room. There was no explaining it, but he had just killed her husband. Although this act saved her daughter's life, she was furious. Bringing her husband's head to her chest, Kaydence held him tight. Blood gushed up from the knife's handle even after his heart stopped pumping, soaking into her shirt.

Officer Alex Martinez was assigned one final mission. That was stopping a fallen angel called Xamreyel from taking over the world. Having Judas inside his head for the brief moment it took to relay this mission was too much for Martinez to handle, but he would not fail. He realized how important it was. And there was no chance in Hell he'd pass up the opportunity to destroy that being that took his partner from him.

Now it was over for Martinez. He knew his time was near, and he welcomed it. There was apology and sorrow in his eyes and they came to rest on Lincoln, who continued to bleed out even though he was dead, and Kaydence, who held him for what may be the last time.

Martinez patiently watched the dead man's wife as she released her husband from her grasp and stood. The look on her face was rage fueled with hatred.

Kaydence flew at him with an amazing amount of speed. Before they collided, he kicked the doll toward Lincoln, where it came to rest at the dead man's feet. Kaydence hit Martinez with enough strength to knock him off balance, but not enough to do what needed to be done. Martinez, however, knew when to play along.

As he fell, in the very brief moment it took to fall, he held tightly onto his friend's hand. Stevens was there beside him, clean-cut and dressed in his finest uniform. Stevens gave him a smile that told him everything was good. And Martinez knew it was. He heard the crunch of bones, the pain was intense, but it was over before he knew it. Every bone in his neck shattered under the weight of his body as he hit the soaking wet ground head first.

Kaydence winced as the body of Officer Martinez hit the ground below Sadie's window. The thump of his body and the rumble of the pouring rain did nothing to hide the loud shattering of his neck. Even the soft, wet dirt did nothing to increase his chances of surviving the drop. A clatter from in the room reminder her that Martinez hadn't been the only threat, she spun quickly around and stared hard at the pastor.

Pastor Simmons didn't give her a chance to channel her anger; after all, Hell hath no fury like a woman scorned. He thought that suited the situation nicely, and without a thought, he worked his way through the busted bedroom door, snagging his jacket briefly on a splinter. He shuffled quickly down the hall, down the stairs, and to the front door. Pulling it open quickly, he burst out into the yard, still holding the knife.

A moment of collective shock washed over the officers outside as the impenetrable house finally opened, and then someone yelled out, "He has a weapon!"

Those were the last words Pastor Simmons heard before the gunshots rang out. It was just one shot at first. Probably a nervous rookie, scared shitless, pulling the trigger out of surprise rather than defense. Then there was a barrage of lead. Blinding bursts of red and blue blended with the orange and white muzzle flashes to create a well-orchestrated fireworks extravaganza. A hero's sendoff which he knew would never be for him. The bullets tore through his soft flesh with ease. The pain was unbearable and he prayed it would be over quick. It was only the beginning of his agony.

Each bright burst from the officer's handguns was like camera flashes, capturing memories that he could now see as the life poured smoothly from his body:

Pastor Simmons, still only a child, sat in the office he now used as his own in the Church of Christ in that sleepy, safe little town of Kathrine, Iowa. His uncle, Jonathan Simmons, a tall man with a well chiseled face and dirty-blond hair, looked down at him with his hypnotic blue eyes. In his hand was a large book with a Literary Classics style cover (dark green with gold designs, squares and triangles from a time long ago) cradling the tattered yellow pages inside, the symbol of the Order of Onyx and Light drawn beautifully in gold leaf.

Uncle Jonathan told him all about his sacred duty: guarding an ancient and holy relic. Young Simmons was thrilled by such a heroic gesture, and he planned on following in his uncle's footsteps. As he grew into a man, he wanted even more to protect that relic, whatever it could be, but not to keep it safe. He wanted to use it to gain power.

A man of God should have everything.

His uncle prepared him to take over the role of guardian, but Uncle Jonathan had no idea his life would end so abruptly. A fatal heart attack took his life at the age of forty-two, and Simmons took over protecting the box and the pestilential being that was held inside. Although he had never opened the box, not from a lack of trying, he was corrupted by the power it contained. He could hear it. He'd heard it for years. It had spoken to him in a loving and nurturing voice.

Bethesda was trapped inside but was able to speak to Pastor Simmons just enough to tell him what must be done. Years of waiting, and the man who could open the box finally came along. He often wondered why it was Lincoln. What made that man, a man without faith, so special? It hardly mattered, anyway. Everything fell into place perfectly. Pastor Simmons was promised unrestrained power. Pastor Simmons was promised eternal life.

Pastor Simmons died face down in the grass, riddled with bullets. Rain fell heavily on his back. Mud caked his thinning hair.

An officer approached the body with his gun drawn cautiously. He knelt down, keeping a watchful eye on the pastor, pressed his index and middle finger into the soft flesh of Pastor Simmons' neck, and confirmed he was dead.

Two other officers crept past and stepped up onto the porch and out of the rain, heading for the open front door. At the moment they reached it, however, it slammed shut. The bang caused a stir among the other officers, as their first instinct was shots fired. Guns were collectively raised.

"What the hell was that?" Sergeant Williams shouted to the officers by the door while he directed an ambulance through the chaos of the yard. The paramedics had been parked at the end of the driveway hoping they wouldn't be needed tonight.

One of the officers at the front door turned to the sergeant and shook his head and gave a confused shrug.

"Sergeant!" a young officer shouted from the corner of the house. "We have an officer down. It's Martinez."

Sergeant Williams raised his bullhorn and started shouting to anyone that was still inside the Scott residents. Many attempts were made to reach the three officers that made it inside, but none of them maintained radio contact. Even with the tremendous volume of the bullhorn, nobody on the inside heard a thing from the outside world, even as officers stood below Sadie's busted window, shouting for the paramedics to help the downed officer.

In Sadie's room, Kaydence lay across Lincoln's body. Her sobs were muffled in his chest. Sadie sat at her father's feet with crossed legs. In her arms, close to her heart, was the doll, Bethesda. Her tear-streaked face was red and puffy.

Sadie wiped her eyes and looked at her father's arms. Black sweat seeped from his skin and began to form a puddle on the floor around him. She called for her mommy, but her gentle, frightened whisper couldn't be heard over Kaydence's sobbing. The black puddle rolled across the floor and grew larger with each drop that oozed from Lincoln's flesh. It circled around his body and vanished under Kaydence.

Once more Sadie tried to call for her mother; once more her mother didn't hear her. Sadie began to feel as if she were just a ghostly presence, long forgotten in an empty house. Nobody could hear her. Than her mother sat up and looked at her. The black sweat crawled up her face and was absorbed into her eyes like an exhaust fan sucking smoke from an overcooked meal on the stove.

"Mommy," Sadie Elizabeth choked. Her voice was a mixture of sadness, confusion, and fear.

"Everything is alright, Sadie," Kaydence said, moving

toward her daughter and pulling the little girl in close. She wrapped her arms tightly around the girl's small body.

"I love you, mommy," Sadie said between sobs.

"I love you, too, sweetie."

The hug steadily became tighter. Before long, Sadie found it hard to breathe. She sucked in a deep breath and waited it out, not wanting to hurt her mother's feelings. She needed comforting now, and Sadie would bear a little pain to provide that comfort. But the pain kept building, and breathing became impossible.

"Mommy, you're hurting me." The words came out in a hoarse whisper.

"It's your fault, sweetie."

Sadie didn't know what she meant or why she was saying it.

"It's your fault your father is dead."

"I'm sorry, mommy." Sadie had no idea what she had done, but she did know that her mother would never lie to her. After all, she trusted that her mommy knew everything.

"I wish you were the one who'd died."

Sadie felt her heart shatter. "I don't want to be dead, mommy. I'm so sorry that I hurt daddy." Speaking through the increasingly tightened grasp of her mother was sending little pops of pain to her throat and chest. She gasped hard for each breath. Lights flashed in her eyes, but she didn't know where they were coming from. Her head began to swim wildly and she was caught in a pained sleepiness. *Mommy*, she begged, but the words only formed in her mind. She no longer had the air to talk.

Kaydence screamed a horrible, cackling scream and dropped Sadie. The air rushing into her little lungs stung just as much as not getting any air had, but she could breathe again, and that is all she cared about. It took her eyes a few seconds to clear the blur, but when they did she saw her mother, writhing in pain on the floor, the screams still split the air.

"Mommy!" Sadie yelled, her voice still hoarse.

The black sweat erupted from Kaydence's nose and mouth but hung in the air as the wet ball grew to the size of a basketball. Kaydence collapsed, breathing heavily and shaking. The black ball hit the floor next to her and cracked open.

The tall charcoal-black figure of Bethesda stood over Kaydence's body. The creature looked down at the woman in disgust before slowly turning toward Sadie. The red eyes were much too large for the figures head. It's once featureless face was now marked with a small nose and wide mouth. Bethesda's jaw unhinged and opened unnaturally wide, revealing two rows of gray teeth. The front row was sharp and scissor-like, while the back was flat and grainy, like small cinderblocks.

A long goatee hung from its chin, a goatee that Sadie would recognize anywhere. It made her question if her father was this terrifying monster. But at the same time, the goatee was not her father's. It squirmed and slithered as if it were made of snakes; like the gorgon, Medusa, only her head had been turned upside down. As it stepped closer to Sadie, she could see that it wasn't snakes, but long black earthworms that looked sticky and mucusy.

Those red eyes stared hard at her. Sadie felt their gaze alone could slice her flesh into thin strips.

"Come to daddy, Sadie." The black monster held its hands out to her and the worms wiggled wildly as if filled with excitement, or laughing wickedly.

"You're not my daddy," Sadie screamed. "Mommy! Mommy wake up!"

Kaydence murmured a little but didn't move.

"Mommy can't help you." Bethesda moved across the room in a blink of an eye and lifted Sadie off her feet. Bethesda's hot breath burned her face, and the stench made her gag. The worms touched her cheeks, leaving behind their excreted mucus.

Edwin watched helplessly as this all happened before him. He was able to interact with Stevens and the pastor, but Bethesda was a much more powerful entity. "You need to stop this! If you can't then you need to tell me how I can," he pleaded, turning to Jesus, who Edwin could tell was growing weaker.

"I'm sorry, Edwin, but there isn't much that we can do."

Jesus replied. "Bethesda was released before we were ready. My strength won't match his until my return to Earth."

"You said I'd get my son back!" Edwin shouted. Son of God or not, Edwin was about to lay into him. "What about God? He's your father, right? Ask Him to put a stop to this. Ask Him to give me my boy back."

"God is not in the position to do that, Edwin. He has many things that require His attention."

"To Hell with you, then. To Hell with God." Edwin turned back to Bethesda. "You can give up, but I won't."

Edwin leapt toward Bethesda. His hand passed through the dry, black flesh—if it could be called that—that covered Bethesda's frame. Just when he thought he would continue passing through the creature, he contacted something inside. It was Lincoln. And with Lincoln was another . . . Adina.

The moment he made contact with them he opened his eyes and was standing in a dark room. The walls and floor were matte black with a hint of red marbling that seemed to slide around the room. The floor was solid, but the walls felt as if they were expanding and contracting around him. He was struck by the feeling that he was inside the lungs of a long-time smoker. There was also a burnt flesh smell that added to the hideous charm of this tar-room.

The only objects Edwin could see were the only ones he cared about at the moment, Lincoln and Adina. Both sat in high-back chairs, their wrists and ankles were bound to the chair by strips of their own flesh, skin hung from their bodies in long bands that looked like loose adhesive tape.

"Lincoln, are you alright?" Edwin asked. His voice seemed to drop in the darkness like a lead sinker on a fishing line.

"Come join us, Edwin," Lincoln said in a friendly manner. He nodded slightly toward a chair next to him that Edwin was sure wasn't there a second ago. "Have a seat, man. You look exhausted."

Edwin was appalled by the smile Lincoln gave him. Half of the man's teeth were rotted and chipped. His tongue was forked.

"Yes, Edwin. Lincoln tells me much about you," Adina said. Her voice was so kind that it shot Edwin's mind back to Sadie.

"Lincoln, snap the fuck out of it, man. You need to help me save your daughter," Edwin urged. He ran to Lincoln and prepared to undo the straps that held his friend in place.

"Please don't do that, Edwin," Lincoln whispered. The man in the chair sounded incredibly sane and fearful.

Edwin looked at Lincoln, looked through him, and saw the friend he'd made so recently yet so completely. "I have to get you out of here, Lincoln."

"If you let me out, I'll kill you. I don't want to do that." Lincoln glanced past Edwin, who followed his eyes.

"Together . . . we can stop this," Jesus said as he and Judas walked up next to Edwin. He looked to Adina and spoke, "I'm so sorry, Adina. I'm going to make everything right by you."

"Please, Jesus. Let me out of here," Adina begged. Her soft voice was filled with terror.

Jesus moved to her and undid her fleshy bindings while Edwin freed Lincoln. Lincoln protested one last time, but Edwin knew everything would be ok with Jesus here.

"What is this place?" Edwin asked.

"It is a dark void deep within Bethesda. I feel weak in here. Even the power of God cannot penetrate the darkness that surrounds us. I'm afraid if our situation worsens, Judas and I will not be much more help than any other mortal man," Jesus responded.

"Thanks for setting us free," Lincoln said, rubbing is wrists where the bindings had dug into his skin. The sanity drained from his voice. "Now you can die!"

Lincoln and Adina burst into a lingering mist that slowly formed into the shape of a dog. Only this dog had red, smoky eyes and a long goatee made of black earthworms. Its forked tongue hung from its mouth, the bottom of the meaty slab being shredded by the sharp teeth, but this didn't seem to bother the creature. Blood trickled out of its maw like a heavy rain.

"Oh shit!" Edwin exclaimed. "Nice doggie." He slowly

backed away holding his hands out in front of him protectively.

The hellbeast snarled ferociously, long black fur stood at attention on its slender back, and jumped unexpected at Jesus who was pushed aside at the last second by Judas. The beast's teeth were bared and ready to rend flesh. Its jaws clamped down tightly and it jerked its head back and forth flinging the man to the ground. Judas cried out in pain as blood gushed from his neck and filled his throat. His gurgled screamed bubbled up, spraying blood across the hellbeast's fur.

Jesus picked himself up from the cold floor where he'd landed. "Judas!" he screamed. He could only watch as his friend's throat and chest were shredded. He turned to Edwin yelled in a commanding voice, "Run, Edwin. You must find a way out of here."

Edwin hesitated for a moment, watching the body of Judas as it was tossed back and forth, and then he ran, but he was unsure of where to go. Everything was black, but he found an opening and walked through it. The next thing he knew he hit the floor of Sadie's room. Bethesda still held the girl, squeezing her.

"Lincoln!" Edwin shouted. "You have to stop this. You are going to kill her. You are going to kill your daughter."

Bethesda turned to Edwin. A hint of regret flashed in those smoky eyes. "I—I am?" Lincoln said sounding slightly lost. "Too bad!" he roared and squeezed the girl even tighter.

Edwin could see that Sadie's gasps were painful, but she also appeared to be too light-headed to notice she was dying. Without a second thought, he dove back into the black, rotten flesh of Bethesda. The hellbeast was still dragging Judas' lifeless body around, the man's head no longer attached to his corpse.

Jesus tried with all his might to pry the dog away from his friend. Blood trickled from a gash in his arm where he was clawed. Prayer ran from his mouth at a mile a minute (far too fast for any mortal ear to comprehend), but they seemed to have little effect here within Bethesda.

Edwin charged in, still running only on instinct. He

wasn't sure if his mind was blank or so full he couldn't sort it all out. He lowered his shoulder like a linebacker and drove right into the hellbeast. There was a sickening crunch from the beast's ribs and a yelp. The earthworms seemed to attempt a vain retreat.

Before the creature could counter, Edwin punched his fist into its red right eye. It squished between his fingers until it burst. Then he grabbed ahold of the thick tendon that was the optical nerve and pulled until it snapped, cracking like a whip. The screams were loud and hideous, fearful and fearless at the same time. The screams came from Edwin as he continued to reach into the empty eye socket of the hellbeast. His fingers scraped against the skull.

Avoided the flailing claws, Edwin pushed his hand in further until he felt something hot and wet with the texture of slimy leather ropes. For the first time since this ruthless attack started, the beast's howls were louder than Edwin's maddened screams. He dug his fingernails into the brain and pulled as hard as he could.

The howls changed pitch spastically. At first they sounded K-9, than more human with bouts of something else entirely. Lincoln's voice broke through before mingling with that of Adina in a horrific collaboration. Edwin, however, continued to dig and pull until the beast's legs stopped thrashing.

After the hellbeast's body stiffened, then went limp, Edwin stood. In his hands was what remained of the creature's brain, squashed in his fingers like gray mashed potatoes. Chunks hit the floor with sickening, sucking *glops*.

"Are you alright?" he asked Jesus. His voice was woozy.

"Yes. Judas will be, as well." Jesus laid his friend's body down and walked toward Edwin.

"Can he be dead? I mean, can—can *we* die?" Edwin asked.

"His pain was real. He suffered, but I will see him again when this is over. It will take time and much strength before he can return." Jesus stared down at the hellhound. Its fur shed in large clumps and flesh melted into a black and red goo as its bulk was slowly absorbed into the floor.

A shudder tore through the room around them. Then everything lurched to the side, knocking the two men off balance. Muffled screams penetrated the walls and seemed to come from all around them.

"I think you weakened it!" Jesus exclaimed. "Come, we must hurry."

They ran toward the black wall and through the small opening that Edwin had found earlier. The blackness was dense and had a weight to it that couldn't be explained. Then Edwin was on the floor of Sadie's room.

XIII

June 13th, 8:50 P.M:

While the police officers outside tried to figure out some way of taking control of the situation, Edwin had already taken a huge step in doing just that. He looked at the black figure of Bethesda as pain rippled visibly through the blackened flesh like a shudder. Sadie was on the floor, gasping and crying and crawling toward her bed. Kaydence was finally coming to, looking around as if she'd woken from a nightmare, and Jesus was nowhere to be found.

As Xamreyel's screams pierced the air, Lincoln stood up as if he were nothing more than a puppet being erected by its puppet master. Seeing this caused Edwin's head to spin, yet with everything he'd experienced it should have been right up there with his new definition of *Fucking Normal*.

Lincoln walked toward Xamreyel, not even glancing at anyone else in the room. Blood pumped from the slash in his chest with each step. His eyes were ablaze with a brilliant blue light. His wrinkled skin was pale and hung loose, but he moved with determination.

Xamreyel knelt and appeared to be fighting off a migraine. "You'll never save her, Son of God! After centuries of imprisonment in that accursed doll, I am still more powerful than He will ever be. And what can you really do to me, anyway? You've already tried exorcism, which is how we arrived to this little predicament in the first place. Plus, you are bound by His weakening power." Xamreyel croaked out a sickened laugh that sounded like a car that won't start.

Lincoln reached down and grabbed ahold of Xamreyel's rough, black neck. Thick black smoke rolled across his eyes, blanketing the bright blue. "I think you have me confused with someone else, fucker."

Xamreyel's red eyes widened, mouth hung agape as if mid-word. A more true form of fear than Edwin had ever seen burned away in those red eyes as he watched Lincoln strangle this demonic fallen angel. The room around them glowed with that eerily calming black light.

"You are a mere mortal. There is no place for you in a world that should be ruled by us!" Xamreyel shouted. "You think *you* can wield God's power better than His own son?"

"I don't need God's power when I have yours," Lincoln said. His words were calm and cold. "*We* . . . have yours," he added as the small figure of Adina appeared next to him. Lincoln felt Xamreyel's power wan as the mortal spirit parted from the demonic fallen angel, leaving only Xamreyel to fight. "Jesus couldn't defeat you without losing Adina because you were smart enough to fuse part of you with her. I set her free, and now your own power will destroy you."

The little girl placed one hand on Xamreyel's chest and picked the doll up off the floor with the other. The little doll's faded eyes burned black and the whole room seemed to have been sucked into a vacuum where no visible light could exist. The temperature fluctuated up and down, jumping a hundred degrees both ways as fast as a child bouncing a rubber ball off the floor.

The erratic fluxes pounding Edwin's senses made him feel as if he would pass out . . . and he was *dead*. He couldn't even imagine what Sadie and Kaydence were feeling, if they were capable of feeling any of it. There was no point trying to check on them. His eyes were glued to Lincoln, Adina, and Xamreyel as they were locked fiercely in a strange battle of stillness. There was something going on that Edwin couldn't see even from whatever plane of existence he was now on.

Lincoln tightened his grip around the throat of Xamreyel, the burnt flaky flesh crumbling between his fingers. His strength, both physical and mental—or maybe it was now spiritual?—drained quickly, but his grip remained. He saw the little hand of Adina as it burned into the blackened chest. A small but steady streamer of smoke rose from between her dirty fingers.

Xamreyel bellowed a cruel, demonic laugh that sent cracks splintering through the walls of the bedroom. Shattering from the hallway chimed into the chaotic orchestra as picture frames fell from their spots on the walls. A long, forked tongue slithered from Bethesda's lips, flickering in the air like a snake's. The long, demonic black wings swept out across the floor. Razor-sharp feathers cut through the rug and sliced into the hardwood flooring, leaving shredded spirals sticking up like wooden corkscrews.

"I sense you, Son of God! You cannot exist here yet, but you're close. Do you want to tell your puppets, or do you even know what you've done?" Xamreyel hissed.

Lincoln's eyes bulged momentarily, and then they contracted inwards. A sharp pain shot through his brain, and he was certain the back of his head would come off, painting the ceiling grayish-red. Crunching in the back of his skull was enough to tell him it wasn't just a feeling: his skull really was about to shatter.

Xamreyel's arm swung out powerfully, batting Adina to the side. The little girl's body flew through the air and slammed into the wall hard, slumping to the ground. She closed her eyes slowly, hoping the pain, or what she felt as pain, would diminish quickly. Struggling, she pulled herself up to her feet. Her legs wobbled under the weight, but then her weight was cut in half.

"Let me help you," Sadie said as she lifted Adina's arm over her shoulder and supported her.

Edwin's body—spirit—had acclimated to the fluctuations in the atmosphere, and he watched Sadie interact with Adina in amazement. He was new to being dead, so he certainly didn't know any of the rules, but seeing a living girl help what he believed to be a ghost to her feet was a bit unexpected. He wondered briefly if she could see him, as well, so he walked quickly toward them. Sadie's eyes shot to him as if she were seeing a shadow out of the corner of her eye, but she didn't focus on him immediately. When she finally did it was as if he had jumped out at her from around the corner.

"Can you see me?" he asked.

"Yes," Sadie responded. She stared at him untrustingly at first before seeming to recognize him. "Can you help my daddy?"

"Yes," he lied. Although he wanted to help, he could feel that whatever power was needed to fight Xamreyel was a power he didn't possess. In fact, just walking closer to Bethesda and Lincoln was taxing. The air around them grew thicker the closer he got. Yet neither seemed effected by whatever it was, as their battle continued on with Lincoln's hand wrapped tightly around Bethesda's throat. Spiritual energy poured out in pulsating waves.

"Can you help that little boy, too?" Sadie pointed toward where Xamreyel and Lincoln were.

"Who?" Edwin looked to where she was pointing and saw Timothy standing beside the blackened, demonic figure. "Timothy." The words came out in a dry whisper that dissipated quickly in the thick air.

The little boy was trapped in the corner of the room by one of Xamreyel's massive wings as it jutted out across the room like a fence. A black wisp reached for Timothy, licking his face and pulling him closer as Xamreyel tried to pull his spirit in and consume whatever power was there. Timothy's screams pelted Edwin's ears like a barrage of mortar rounds.

Edwin took off toward his son, ignoring the battling figures. The air quickly grew too thick to move through, but he kept moving his legs, inching forward, allowing the frightened screams of Timothy to fuel a whole new rage inside him. The screams grew ear-splittingly loud before Edwin realized that he was also screaming. Timothy was just within reach when Xamreyel's wing shot up, colliding with Edwin's face and tossing him back several feet.

"Edwin!" Lincoln shouted. "You have to trap this beast in the doll!"

"It won't work! Xamreyel cannot be drawn into the doll without a mortal soul to act as a tether." Edwin was shocked as the words came out. He wasn't sure how he knew that, but he felt it was true. "Lincoln! I'm sorry, but that means—"

"I know what it means," Lincoln sighed. He looked away from Xamreyel, locking his eyes on Timothy. The terror on the boy's face was heart-wrenching. Lincoln wondered if Edwin and Timothy would have a chance to live out their lives.

Then he looked past Edwin to his own child. Sadie Elizabeth stood with a determined look on her face as she held up Adina, Kaydence stood by her on the other side. There was also fear in their faces, and the desire to go home, to them, was far too great to ignore. A hot tear rolled down his face, searing a red trail into his cheek.

Finally he turned his attention to Edwin. The man continued to fight his way through whatever barrier Xamreyel had in place. For a second Lincoln's eyes met Edwin's. Power surged through both men as a spiritual link was created. The link was fragile, but it was there, and Lincoln smiled as Edwin took a big step toward him, reached down to pick up the doll, and took another step.

Lincoln loosened his grip on Xamreyel's neck and instantly felt wave after wave of the demon's energy cut through him. Each blast was like a nausea-inducing shock that rocketed past his exterior and pummeled his insides. His teeth vibrated, a few even fell from their sockets. A cloudy white cataract developed over his pupils.

"You will not beat me, mortal," Xamreyel claimed. Confidence swelled from the fallen angel. "I am far too strong. My power cannot be contained in such a frail object any longer. I may have lost the girl for now, but after I take you there will be nobody to stop me!"

"I let you control me once, but it isn't happening again. I am stronger than you!" Lincoln shouted. "I am stronger than you!"

Edwin reached them and stretched his arm out toward Xamreyel. The little doll began to smolder in his hand, and he was certain it would burst into flames, but if catching fire is what it took to save his son than he would gladly suffer. A long curved splinter stabbed through his leg as Edwin dropped to his knees. The wood scrapped against his kneecap hard enough to carve out the bone.

His pained screams were drowned out by Lincoln's, whose skin had tightened over his muscles to the point of stretching, and eventually splitting. The sound was like tearing cloth: an action hero ripping his sleeve off to bandage a wound. Blood pattered down in thick, coagulated raindrops that were absorbed by Xamreyel's burnt flesh. Each drop making the black creature stronger.

"You will never win, Son of God!" Xamreyel screamed. Those smoky marble eyes darted around the room. Jesus was close, watching over a scene he could no longer control, but the demonic orbs couldn't lock onto him. "I will be victorious, and when I am, I will bring the full might of Hell raining down on your little sanctuary. Heaven will fall!"

Lincoln felt Xamreyel's mental assault weaken slightly. There was some doubt brought on by his lack of experience in dealing with demons, or fallen angels as circumstances would have it, but he felt confident that now was his best chance at doing whatever it was he had to do. Lincoln opened up his mind, hoping that was what it took to open his soul, and leaned forward into Xamreyel, whose marble eyes widened.

"You're mine now, motherfucker!" Lincoln whispered. His flesh, already torn and bloody, began to peel away in strips as he fought his way closer to Xamreyel. He dug his fingers into the black chest and pulled himself in.

As the two bodies met, Lincoln felt pain unlike anything he'd ever imagined. Every molecule in his flesh erupted. Blood sprayed around the room, covering everything in a fine mist. The pain was so intense that Lincoln couldn't even scream. Xamreyel, however, shrieked.

All that was left of Lincoln's flesh was the grotesque fold that was once his bottom lip, but it was also dripping away like melted wax. His body resembled a medical poster of the muscular system. It wasn't long before his muscle tissue started to snap, breaking apart like taut strings or old rubber bands. He started to feel as if he were trapped between a wall and a boulder that kept grinding slowly into him.

He turned and starred at his wife and daughter. They were so beautiful, and God was he going to miss them. If there was ever a time to pray, it was now, and he opened his mind up even further and prayed for their safety. He prayed that whatever the hell he was doing was going to work. Lincoln focused one last time on his girls, praying they didn't have to look so scared.

Then a new pain exploded in his eyes. He tried to blink it away, but his eyelids were gone. He imagined it was what a person would feel if their eyes were ripped out and ground down with sandpaper. His mouth hung open, but there was still no sound coming out. His lungs popped like over-inflated balloons, sending blood spraying from his mouth. He was now lying perfectly on top of Xamreyel. Their legs were already beginning to meld together. Next, their chest connected, and finally, Lincoln was able to press his skinless face down against Xamreyel's.

All of the pain vanished, and Lincoln sat up. At first he thought it was all a dream, but that thought only fired off for a split second before he realized he wasn't in control anymore. A thick layer of confusion brushed over his mind, than he realized there was another mind next to his that also fought off this brief moment of uncertainty.

Oh shit, Lincoln thought as he realized he was inside Xamreyel. He looked toward his feet and saw Edwin knelt down with the doll, unsure of how to use it.

"Edwin!" Lincoln shouted as Xamreyel stood up. He felt as if he was on a theme park ride were he had no control over what was happening. "Edwin, you need to trap us in the doll!"

But Edwin didn't hear any of this.

"You will join your son, Edwin." Xamreyel stated. "You will be allowed to burn beside him for eternity."

Edwin released a scream like a mighty battle-cry and leapt forward, knocking Xamreyel off balance. The winged monster stumbled backward before recuperating. Edwin charged forward again before Xamreyel was ready. This time they both fell to the floor where Edwin held the doll over the demon's head.

The doll burned hotter, smoke rolled from the linen and straw but Edwin held tight. He balled his right hand into a fist and drove it repeatedly into Xamreyel's head. He was sure this didn't help the situation, but it sure as hell made him feel better. As the doll continued to burn, Edwin could feel his palm blister. Those blisters popped, sending pus seeping through his fingers.

Xamreyel reached a hand up and grabbed Edwin's neck. The strong fingers closed tightly, but Edwin remained calm, knowing he didn't need to breathe anyway. But that didn't help him overcome the pressure that caused his eyes to bulge until the right one broke open like a piñata, spraying its contents. Even dead, the pain was extraordinary.

Lincoln watched helplessly from inside Xamreyel's head. His mind fumbled around, hoping to come across some way of helping. He mentally reached out, trying to take control of the demon's arms or loosen the grip on Edwin's neck, but he couldn't seem to do anything. Feeling useless, Lincoln gave up.

"After I'm finished with you, your son will know what true pain is!" Xamreyel roared.

Edwin held the doll against Xamreyel's face and watched through his good eye as the black flesh was pulled into the little linen doll. Xamreyel looked back into Edwin's face and gave the man a smile before squeezing his neck even tighter. The world around Edwin went black as the other eye popped, but the pain only lasted a second. Xamreyel twisted Edwin's neck with one powerful motion and tossed the man's limp body aside.

Lincoln screamed as he watched Edwin and the doll hit the floor. This made Xamreyel laugh a dominant, crazed laugh.

"Now the rest of you will feel pain like you've never imagined possible." Xamreyel wings stretched from wall to wall.

"NO!" This time Lincoln's scream escaped Xamreyel's lips, and the large creature took a step back toward Edwin's body.

"You are not powerful enough to control me!" Xamreyel bellowed. Surprise filled the smoky eyes as Lincoln took two more steps, reached down with Xamreyel's left hand, and picked up the doll.

"You don't belong here, demon!" Lincoln yelled. "And you sure as hell won't touch my family."

He held up the doll and pressed it firmly into Xamreyel's chest. Pain shot through Xamreyel's body that both of them felt. Flakes of burnt flesh evaporated into a fine black smoke as it reached the doll. The smoke rolled into Bethesda's pale eyes as if it were being sucked away by an exhaust fan. Lincoln and Xamreyel screamed as one as the body that was now theirs dispersed.

Lincoln tried to tell Kaydence and Sadie that he loved them, but the words wouldn't come out. He reached a grotesque black hand out to them, but this only frightened them, as neither was completely sure of what they were seeing. Kaydence wrapped her arms protectively around Sadie. Only Adina waved goodbye.

Bethesda dropped to the floor, smoking profusely. The centuries old straw and linen caught fire quickly. It burned hot and fast. In less than a minute, the doll was ashes.

Adina walked across the room, stepping over the blackened spot on the floor and reached out for Timothy to take her hand. Timothy looked sadly at her, but she gave him a smile that assured him everything would work out. Together they walked over to Sadie.

"I am terribly sorry this has happened to you. Never forget your father's sacrifice," Adina said.

"I won't," Sadie replied. She rubbed away her tears with her arm.

"You won't what, honey?" Kaydence asked, wiping away her own tears.

"It's time for us to go," Adina said to Timothy.

They walked across the room to the door and vanished as they crossed over.

"Can you hear that, mommy?" Sadie asked as the sounds of the police outside spilled in through the open window.

"Come with me and stay low, ok?"

"Ok, mommy."

Kaydence led Sadie out into the hallway and down the stairs. Through the living room window she could see an officer peering in, his handgun held at his side. She waved to the officer to show him they were unarmed and coming out. He nodded and shouted to the other officers to hold their fire.

The door opened slowly and Kaydence stepped out first. Sadie was close behind. The officer at the window came over to them and lifted the little girl up in his arms and guided them through the maze of police cruisers to where an ambulance waited.

"Are you alright, ma'am? What happened in there?" Sergeant Sean Williams asked. He climbed into the back of the ambulance beside them and out of the softening rain.

"I—I don't really know," Kaydence replied. Her mind jumped back and forth as it tried to comprehend any of what they had just been through.

"There is nobody else in the house, ma'am. Is there another way out?" the sergeant asked coolly.

"Just the backdoor and the garage," she answered without looking at him.

"Ok. We're going to send you both to the hospital for an evaluation. Once there you two just get some rest, and I'll come by and check on you in a day or two." Sergeant Williams stepped out of the ambulance, closed the door, and pounded on the side.

"Hey, Sarge. We searched everywhere. There is nobody else here. We had the place surrounded and there are no other exits or tunnels we can find," the officer from the window said as he walked beside the sergeant.

"Well they sure as hell didn't vanish! There has to be a hiding place in there somewhere." Sergeant Williams didn't take his eyes off the ambulance until it was out of sight.

"Do you think they were in on this?" the officer asked. He nodded at the ambulance as it drove off down the driveway.

"I don't know, but I want you to follow them to the hospital. And don't let them out of your sight when you get there. I'll assign a few officers to their room when they get settled in."

"Yes, sir," the officer said. He jogged through the mud to his cruiser and drove off after the ambulance.

A paramedic sat in the back of the ambulance with Kaydence and Sadie as they rolled at a comfortable cruising speed toward the hospital in Muscatine. The paramedic was an older man with a gentle voice that Sadie found to be very comforting. He asked several questions, but Kaydence only answered in short, choppy sentences that didn't seem to bother the man at all. In fact, he preferred it that way knowing how delicate situations ending in an ambulance ride could be.

Sadie looked down at her hands. She wasn't sure if the water droplets landing in her palms were from the rain in her hair or the tears in her eyes. There was no way for her to fully understand what had happened, but she knew that she would now be living the rest of her life without her father. Looking out through the small rear window of the ambulance she watched her house disappear into the night.

It was at the exact moment her home blinked out of existence into the night that her life fully changed. What had happened was far beyond her comprehension. There was, however, hope.

Hope...and faith.

Epilogue

The navy-blue fabric of the skirt suit clung to the curves of the new pastor's body a little more than the women liked, but the men didn't mind. The men, of course, wouldn't admit that to their wives to save their souls knowing that it would bring more pain and suffering than anyone could experience in Hell. Yet it was the men who'd argued against a woman pastor when she took over just a few weeks ago.

Her high heels clicked and clacked on the concrete with each determined step she took. Her sermon had ended and the churchgoers that hung around for chit-chat had departed. She enjoyed hanging out with the people who came to her for spiritual guidance. She also knew that right now she was still meeting new people, and everyone was excited to hear what she had to say, no matter how mundane it may be.

It was late August in that small Iowa town of Kathrine. The sky was growing dark. A storm was rolling in. The cool breeze carried with it the smell of rain. Not just a good sprinkle, but a downpour. The last few months had seen an unusual number of storms; at least that's what the weather man on Channel 6 had said all week.

An Unusual number of them no doubt.

Click—Clack—Click—Clack

The pastor's long black hair danced around her face as the wind picked up. The latest gust carried with it a chill that wasn't associated with the incoming cold front. There was something more to it, something that gave her goosebumps.

Footsteps from behind her caused her to stiffen slightly. There were very few things in this world that scared her, and most of those things didn't originate on earth.

"Excuse me, Pastor," a deep voice called smoothly from behind her. There was something soothing in the voice, but her senses told her not to drop her guard.

The pastor turned slowly, staring hard at the man walking toward her. He was a tall black man with a large smile. He was dressed in black button-up shirt with the white clerical collar and black slacks. As he approached she could see the kindness in his eyes. He appeared to be in his late thirties, his black hair carried the first signs of graying around the temples. In his right hand was a book, which she presumed to be a bible with a sky blue cover.

"Can I help you?" she asked.

"No. I can help you, however."

She didn't respond to this. Instead she glanced at him with a look of slight impatience.

He glanced around as if sensing the same unearthly chill that she had sensed earlier. "Is there somewhere we can talk?"

"Here is fine," she replied. Her voice was stern. Just because this man showed up dressed as a priest didn't mean she'd trust him.

Sensing, and completely understanding her distrust, he obliged, "Of course. I was sent because I don't like to beat around the bush, as they say, so here it is: We understand you have a close connection with the Order of Onyx and Light."

She interrupted him before he could say any more, "The Onyx Light is a myth."

"Is it?" His eyes said she was wrong, and they showed truth.

"Who are you? Who are *we*?" She asked.

"Sadie Elizabeth Scott. Nineteen years ago your father died destroying an evil entity known as Xamreyel and freeing a little girl named Adina from that entity."

Sadie's eyes widened in surprise. "You must not read the paper. They said my father was a murderer. Killed several people then set himself on fire. There was nothing left. My mother and I just barely escaped."

"You know that isn't true. Is that really what you've allowed others to believe?" he asked.

"It's what they *have* to believe," Sadie replied. There was pain in the words.

The priest only nodded his agreement.

"Besides," she continued, "If I had told what really happened I'd probably still be locked away in Mireside."

He nodded in agreement again, this time with a soft smile on his face.

"What do you want exactly? You said you could help me. Help me with what?" It was time to cut the shit.

"There's something coming. You've felt it as much as we have. Maybe more. We need the Onyx Light."

"The Onyx Light died with my father and Xamreyel," Sadie stated.

"Then why did you rewrite the book?"

There was another jolt Sadie didn't expect.

The priest continued, "You came back here for one thing: To find the book of the Onyx Light written by Pastor Simmons. You found it. You rewrote it. You've become the Guardian of the Onyx Light. The only one left, and with Xamreyel gone . . . you don't have a cause. We can give you a cause."

"You're correct about one thing: Xamreyel has been defeated, and Xamreyel was the whole purpose for the Order of Onyx and Light. The reason I came back here is because the Onyx Light must always shine. I'm not a demon hunter. I'm not an exorcist. I'm not whatever you and whoever the hell *we* is are looking for. I want to be left alone."

Sadie walked to the fully restored 34 Ford Coupe that used to belong to her father and climbed in. After sliding the key into the ignition she rolled up the sleeves of her blouse. Both arms were covered in tattoos. Three crucifixes at Calvary Hill were in black and shades of gray on her left forearm. Her right arm displayed Jesus with the crown of thorns upon his head.

She looked at the priest still standing in the parking lot twenty yards behind her. He gave no sign that he would pursue her anymore.

The powerful 302 came to life with a wicked growl that cackled through the chrome side-pipes. Sadie wrapped her fingers around the pistol grip shift knob and pressed the clutch. The transmission slid into first gear smoothly. She couldn't help but light up the tires as she pulled out of the parking lot. There were numerous black marks that everyone seemed to ignore. Someday someone would ask her who was doing it, but for now she didn't care.

The Coupe rumbled down the street, catching the eye of everyone she drove by even though they all had seen it before. It was just one of those cars that turned heads. That's what it was built for.

Pulling off the street, she popped the transmission into neutral and coasted down the long driveway. She had owned the property for three years. Taking it over when her mother passed away. She had no husband or children to share the large house and yard with, but she liked being secluded.

Climbing out of the hot rod, she stared at the house. She always did when she got home for the day; ritual or habit, she didn't know. Either way, she was home. Like her car, the door to her house always remained unlocked. There was never any serious crime in this town, and if there was she really wouldn't care.

The house was empty. All she had was a table, couch, bed, and a few chairs.

After a hot shower, she wiped the layer of moisture from the mirror and stared into her father's eyes. They were her eyes, of course, but they were the only part of her that reminded her of him. Every other feature she had come from her mother. But that was fine by her; she always thought her mother was beautiful.

On her naked back was another tattoo. It was of a woman with her arms wrapped protectively around a little girl. Darkness crept up all around them. Light tore down in bright streams from between her shoulder blades. Inside the light was a man with a long goatee hanging from his smiling face. His eyes were kind. He aimed the light into the darkness, pushing it back and lighting the way for his wife and daughter.

After dressing in jean shorts and a loose-fitting t-shirt, she grabbed her bible—a large leather-bound book with pages gilded in gold leaf—and headed out to the garage. Opening the door she reached along the garage wall and flicked on the lights. Although it was still early afternoon the storm clouds cast an eerie darkness on the world.

The rusty blue Chevy pickup sat in the far bay in the

same condition her father had left it. She walked across the concrete floor, reached out her hand, and ran her fingers along the rough paint under the window.

On the seat of the Chevy was a book she'd never seen before. Wait. She had seen it. It was the sky blue bible the priest had been carrying. Quickly, she spun around looking for any signs of an intruder. Moving to the wall she grabbed a large wrench and wielded it like a barbarian would a club.

"God might not approve of me busting your head open, but I will if I must." She backed herself along the wall where no attack could come from behind. Luckily for her the garage was large and open. There was only the Chevy, so it took only a few minutes to confirm she was alone.

Walking back to the truck she pulled the passenger's side door open, reached in, and grabbed the book that rested on the seat. The cover was made of a thin leather with shallow ridges. The sky blue coloring was far more brilliant up close. The pages were dry and slightly yellowed.

The pages were also blank.

Sadie flipped the hefty book around in her hands several times, examining the exterior. Opening the book, she examined the blank yellow pages. The sweet aroma of being deep in a library escaped the pages as she thumbed through them on her search for some clue as to what this book was for.

"*You* can help *me* by giving me a purpose?" she scoffed. "And you give me an empty book."

She let a sigh escape her that was part laugh and part confused amazement at the audacity of some people. The book smacked against the seat of the Chevy as she tossed it back down. She closed the door hard and walked across the garage to the door into the house. Turning back she looked at the truck and thought of the book on the seat. *Blank*, she thought. *So I can write my own story.*

"Or the story *we* want me to write."

She opened the door between the garage and the house, reached an arm along the garage wall, and flicked off the lights before closing the door behind her.

ABOUT THE AUTHOR

D.L. Spitznogle is an IT professional who lives in Southern California with his wife, Kortnie, and their three children. As a fan of horror, D.L. Spitznogle has always wanted to create stories that will terrify, excite, and motivate readers. He began his writing career under the pen name Linus Locke with the Decay: stories, and he has stated that Linus still has stories to share.

www.LinusLocke.com
www.Facebook.com/AuthorLinusLocke
www.twitter.com/linuslocke

Made in the USA
Monee, IL
23 April 2022

95254951R00108